THE CHEROKEE PRINCESS AND THE BLOODWOOD FLUTE

Lurlynn L. Potter

ISBN: 978-1-968397-07-4
First Edition
Published by Viral Book Nation
Albany, New York, USA

This is a work of fiction. Names, characters, places, and incidents are either the product of the author's imagination or used fictitiously. Any resemblance to actual persons, living or dead, or actual events is purely coincidental.

TABLE OF CONTENTS

Chapter I
Jerusalem

Ziven let out a long sigh, smiled and shook her head, her eyebrow raised and her golden-green eyes rolling ever-so-slightly. The young boys had obviously done something they knew they shouldn't have and were running before they could get caught. Most likely, they had stolen some candied figs or dates. Their bare feet slapped against the cobblestone streets and their breathless giggling echoed through the corridors of the narrow stone passageways. Chickens squawked and struggled to get out of their way as they ran quickly past, darting around street vendors and people who were clearly in their way. Their heads swung from side to side and their eyes scanned for any followers. Laughing wildly, they disappeared into an alleyway and faded away as quickly as they had appeared.

Ziven smiled as she touched her abdomen. She loved children, and had waited so long for this moment. Thirty years seems like an eternity when you are waiting for something you desperately desire. The emotional ups and downs almost destroyed her marriage. Each month seemed to be filled with desperation, hope, denial, discouragement, and resignation. A relentlessly repeating cycle that left her sometimes feeling numb; at other times, the sensory overload put her into a deep depression that closed her off from everyone and everything that had meaning in her life. She thought her mother would understand, but instead, she felt an added pressure from her family and society in general, that seemed to put a very private torture under a magnifying glass for all to gossip about, or question her about ruthlessly.

Finally, at long last, she had succeeded! Like the olive trees all around her, she would finally bear fruit. Would it be a boy, like these boys in the streets, who would most likely learn to steal, or go to war; or would it be a girl who would have to fight for an education and hide any fire or spunk she might inherit from her mother? What would growing up in Jerusalem be like for her child? What would the world be like for her? Could she be happy growing up in a culture that forces women to hide behind tradition and walk behind men? Or, if it is a boy, could he be happy growing up in fear of bombs, killing, and war training?

Her smile was quickly replaced by a furrowed brow. *These are hard times,* Ziven thought to herself, *but I guess all times are hard.* The history of her people has always seemed to be filled with turmoil and unrest. How ironic that the greeting everyone uses daily is "Shalom" which means: peace, harmony, completeness, prosperity, healing, and tranquility... yet is used so universally among a people whose existence has been anything but those things.

She looked out the window at the cobblestone streets and the seemingly endless jungle of concrete buildings with fragile red tile roofs, and let her mind drift comfortably to the days – not so long ago – when she was a child on the streets of Jerusalem.

It was springtime – those fleeting 2-3 weeks when even the cracks in the sidewalks seem to come alive. Blood-red poppies seem to find their way into any piece of earth and triumphantly burst upward in full bloom at the same time each year. For Ziven, it was as though she could hear them singing in exultant joy. A musical chord seemed to reverberate from every living thing at that time more than usual. The warm, solid tones sung by the blossoming almond trees, the tinkling melodic sounds of the new grass, and the joyful shouts of the lilies of the field (or red poppies) filled Ziven's heart with a happiness she knew she could never explain to another human being.

A thunderstorm rolled in with its dark billowing cumulus clouds and flat shaded bottoms that threatened to drench everything below in a matter of minutes. Ziven loved to stand in an open field at times like that, so she could feel the power of the wind. She loved to be "at one" with nature. Her favorite thing to do as a child was to sit all alone in a meadow with bread crumbs enticing small creatures to surround her. She always felt such peace and joy at times like that. They always communicated such love for her. She could sense their emotions and share with them a sense of peace and love from deep within herself. She could transmit these messages to all creatures, always has been able to.

But a thunderstorm was just as wonderful as a moment like that. She loved how the trees bent and danced with the wind. It was almost magical. She could hear them praising their creator and laughing as they swayed back and forth. Every cell in her body could feel the electricity and the power of such storms. She knew there was a God, and felt herself swirling joyously within the majesty of nature much like a falling leaf swirls in the wind.

As usual, Ziven would find a large Carob tree to climb into. Trees are perfect for reading... or for spying! She loved the chocolaty smell of the seed pods, and the way the trees seemed to welcome her into their branches. It was then that she learned that not everyone can sense the thoughts of plants and trees as she could. Somehow, she had always been able to, so it felt simply natural to her.

Two women were walking down the street with children in their arms, and each was also skillfully balancing a basket of freshly purchased food for the day. Their many layers of brightly-colored clothing and ornately decorated scarves lined with glimmering gold designs gave away their religious sects. They were Orthodox Jews; one Open, and the other Modern. It was not unusual for women of varying sects to be friends. *"Anything is possible in Jerusalem,"* Ziven had told herself.

Indeed, Jerusalem is the center of the religious world. Christians, Jews, and Islam all claim Jerusalem as their holy land... the center and beginning of their faith. Although Jewish guards usually stand guard at every major intersection, peace is generally maintained and all faiths occasionally live in peace together. It is a delicate balance that goes back and forth between being volatile and peaceful at a moment's notice; just like the weather on the hills of Judea.

As Ziven remained hidden in the Carob (or Locust) tree, the chattering voices of the two women reached her and she heard her name. "... little Ziven, who thinks she can hear the flowers and the trees! Why, she would probably talk to these vegetables in our baskets and tell them not to let us eat them!" It wasn't so much what they said, but the laughter that followed that deeply hurt her feelings.

Ziven could feel her face get hot and the tears start to flow uncontrollably from her large hazel eyes. As the first salty tear drop landed on the branch of the tree that had lent its arms for her support, she could hear it say to her, *"Little one, why cry because you are more loved?"* She answered, *"What do you mean, more loved?"* She felt the reply, *"It is a gift to be at one with nature... a talent and an honor."* Ziven thought for a moment, then asked the tree, *"Why me?"* Then she felt a booming laughter and, *"Why not you? You are special. You are chosen."*

The words the tree used for "special" and "chosen" seemed synonymous with "set apart" and "different." Yes, Ziven knew she was "different." She had always known that about herself. It wasn't so much that the teasing boys would chant, "Ziven is a weirdo! Ziven is a weirdo!" (in Hebrew of course), but Ziven had always found a strange, secret delight in being peculiar. She never enjoyed the same things most girls her age liked to do either. She wasn't interested in playing three-sticks, or dressing dolls. If she could do anything in the world, it would be to climb high into a tree and read. Her favorite thing to read about was America, and the Native Americans who lived there before it became "The United States of America."

One day, quite by accident, Ziven had found a peculiar pink plastic bracelet in her mother's chest she had been rummaging through. It had the inscription *"1962-04-01 Gwenelda. Cherokee"* on it. It was too large to belong to a doll's arm, but too small for a person... maybe a baby's wrist? It had been cut off... Curious.

Ziven will never forget the look on her mother's face when she asked her about it. Almost at once the emotions of surprise, fear, and resolve flashed across the beautiful olive complexion and dark brown eyes of the face Ziven had only known as "Ima" (or Mother). After taking a deliberate, deep breath (her courage gathered), she began.

"You were not born of Jewish blood," her ima began slowly. "I am... barren." With that, she quickly looked up to meet her daughter's gaze.

Ziven's mother had long thick ebony-colored hair that shone with mahogany highlights in the sun. She was a beautiful woman, but the twinkle in her eye was gone as she explained that she and her husband had anguished many years over not being able to have children together. The weight of the burden of shame was almost too heavy to bear as she revived those painful days.

A Jewish woman who could not bear children was looked upon as "cursed" by God, and was often not included in social events or community celebrations. She had known what it was like to be an outcast in her synagogue, and an outcast in the community; whispered about and ignored as though she were invisible. The weight of the burden of shame was almost too heavy to bear as she revived those painful days.

Antje regained her composure and took a deep breath as her grimace left and her features softened. She smiled gently at her little girl. "Then the LORD gave us a most precious gift," she continued. The twinkle was back in her eyes as she leaned in and smiling said, "He gave us YOU!" Ziven's ima told her about the day when she and "Aba" had found a baby in the rubble of an orphanage in the Gaza strip that had been bombed with mortar fire by religious extremists. They had fallen in love with her instantly and decided to call her "Ziven" which is Hebrew for "alive" because she alone survived. Truly a gift from JEHOVAH.

Ziven took inventory. Her skin was slightly lighter than her parents, but darkened easily as she played upon the tiled rooftops of the concrete village in the warm dry sun. Her skin, when darkened by the sun, had a reddish tint to it though – which was unusual. And during the cooler months when Ziven was not outside as much, her skin still remained olive-colored. This dark skin was set off by her golden-hazel eyes and light brown hair that grew blonder as she spent more time outside in the summer months. Her nose certainly looked Jewish, but she had high cheek bones and short eye lashes; traits she had reluctantly grown to accept. She knew in her heart that what her ima was telling her was true. She truly was "different."

Then, she asked, "So, what does *Gwenelda Cherokee* mean and where did this pink 'bracelet' come from?" Her ima smiled, "I thought you might ask me that someday! You were wearing that pink bracelet when we found you. After much study, I learned that in America, the Native American people who called themselves 'Cherokee' were a noble and intelligent people. They had their own written language, government, and were a peace-loving people, unlike many of the other Native American people at that time. We Jews have much in common with them. I believe 'Gwenelda' was your birth name. It is a Cherokee word that means 'princess.' So, you see, you are a 'Cherokee Princess'."

Before letting that sink in, she asked, "and the numbers?" "That, my love, is your true birth date. Today you have 8 years," replied Antje.

Ziven thought about that for a moment. She wondered what happened to her birth parents. She wondered how she came to be in an orphanage in the Gaza strip. She wondered if her parents were still alive, and if they ever thought of her or wondered what had happened to her. She wondered if they thought she was dead. So many questions. No answers. At least not now. Somehow Ziven felt inside that she would someday find the answers to these questions. A peaceful feeling drenched her body like a warm summer's rain. Somehow, she knew she would discover where she came from and what she was meant to do. She just had to be patient and ready to act when the time came.

"*That was long ago,*" she thought to herself, coming back to the present. "*So much has changed. I have changed. I am not sure of anything anymore. My life is so uncertain. I may never find any answer to any of my questions... And I certainly don't feel like a 'Princess'!*"

Chapter II
Deep in a Forest in South America

I sing praise that I live! I sing praise that there is water at my roots! I draw the nutrient-rich moisture up through my roots with ease. I am grateful for deep roots and fertile soil beneath me. I feel joy when the warm sunlight shines on my limbs and leaves. They tingle as the energy flows through them. I shout songs of praise and thanks to my Creator!

I feel solid and strong. I sing praise!

There is a young evergreen tree growing near my base. It grows so very slowly. It needs my protection, and my help. I must move my trunk ever-so slightly to let more delicious sunlight in. I will lean a little bit every day. I sing praise that I can serve this little tree! I shout praise that I can give!

Today I was injured by a deer who was sharpening its antlers. Their fuzzy velvet must itch terribly for the deer to feel the need to rub them on me. My blood-red sap flows freely from the wound. But I am not sorrowful, I sing praise that I live! I sing praise that I could offer my help to such a beautiful and noble creature!

The wind blows through my branches and leaves and makes me dance. I feel to dance a song of praise to my Creator! I will sing praise as I dance in delight! Praise and joy!

I stretch to find more sunlight, and dig my roots deeper in search of fresh living water. My veins tingle when the sparkling, singing water makes its way upward to my branches. Then, when the warm sunlight soaks into my leaves, I feel energized and alive. When the light reaches the living water, it is like an explosion of joy! I sing praise even louder to my Creator!

Every day is a celebration! The warm moist air is comfortable for thousands of varieties of insects and other creatures. Every living thing joins me in singing songs of praise to the Creator! What a glorious symphony! The beautiful Toucans and Macaws call out to the world. The squeaks and howls of the monkeys and lemurs are haunting in the shadows of the deep forest. Even the slow deep tones of the sloth support the songs from the upper canopy.

I notice, on the forest floor, that everything is alive. Even the decaying leaves that have fallen from my branches still have enough life in them to sing praise. The turtles, frogs, and snakes, creeping things and other forms of animal life all go about living to the measure of their creation. The very elements of their souls are in a constant state of singing and praising their Creator.

The water creatures and the life within the soil sing a different song, but it is in beautiful concert with the music of the rain forest. Life and death are in a delicate balance, and every moment is precious to that balance. The songs of those creatures is more passionate and full of emotion. It is a song that they sing all day and all night, every day... day after day. They are filling the measure of their creation. They are feeling joy and rejoicing! That's why they sing.... They are filling and feeling the measure of their creation!

I wonder what the measure of MY creation is?

I noticed today that it is helping the young sapling for me to lean and twist. It is becoming strong and is growing straight and tall. Someday, it may make a beautiful tree: tall and straight. I feel happy to help.

A man came into the forest today. He was cutting many of my family trees. He was removing their branches and carrying them away. It looked like a blood bath as the deep red sap poured out of the remaining trunks.

No cries of pain were heard, but a new silence seems to grow. There are less of my family singing praise with me. The wise old tree told me this day would come. I learned many years ago to trust the wisdom of the oldest among us. Now the wise one has been carried away, and I am left to take his place. I am now the oldest. Does that make me the wisest? This I do not know, but I do know this; I must protect the little ones. And, I must continue to sing praise!

———

I must have been singing praise too loudly to hear the man return. Before I knew it, he had sliced into my strong trunk with a metal blade! My blood-red sap poured freely and I felt light leave my branches. I felt no pain, but only a curious sensation of numbness. I was no longer connected to light, no longer connected to life!

Am I... dead?

———

I still sing praise, but it is different. My songs don't seem to rise into the air around me as freely. Is this the way it feels for all of my family who have been cut and carried away? I can no longer communicate with them. I will continue to sing praise to my Creator because I live... at least I think I live. I wonder if the other trees laying beneath me are alive. I cannot see their light, and I cannot hear their songs of praise. Surely, they are still singing... I just cannot hear them any longer. I will sing for all of us. I must sing louder.

———

I am having trouble remembering what it is like to be in the beautiful living forest. I am at a loss to imagine what is in my future. I cannot drop any *more seeds. I cannot provide any shade. I cannot sing songs of praise! I cannot help anyone. I cannot serve. What will happen to the little Evergreen tree if I am not there to protect it? Who will be the 'wise one' now?*

Something is wrong, terribly wrong! Am I alive? I20 will try to sing a song of praise... I must try.

I feel the sun warming my trunk, but the light is slow to soak in. I feel so very dry. I cannot move. There is no wind dancing through my branches. No living water to parch my thirst. No animals to protect. No service to give. What will become of me? I must sing songs of praise to my Creator... even if He cannot hear me any longer. I must sing! I must try to sing... I feel tired. I feel sad and sleepy. But more than that, suddenly, I feel cold. I feel cold, and alone.

I hear a sound that is unfamiliar. It vibrates my veins... that is if I still have veins. I am being sliced and cut into sharp-edged pieces! Surprisingly, it doesn't hurt as I am being cut off, but it does make me feel very sleepy. It feels different from the slumber of winter. I can feel the last of my deep red "sap" draining from my "veins" and I wonder if I will ever awaken. I feel so heavy!

How will I ever sing praises now? How can I ever serve? How can I ever give now? I feel so very dry and hard... I feel 'different.'

These were the last thoughts the Blood Wood Tree had before sinking deeply into a sleep with no dreams.

Chapter III
Purim

The days of Purim were upon her, and Ziven had much to prepare. She thought of Queen Esther who had made preparations to gain the king's favor before asking him to spare the Jews. This was the reason for Purim celebration. Ziven had always loved the story of Esther. She had imagined what she would have done if she had been Queen Esther.

Queen Esther was a Jewish maiden who was chosen as the successor to the queen of Persia because of her profound beauty. When she discovered that her people—the Jews—were to be put to death, she risked her own life by going to the king without being summoned. This was unheard of; unprecedented!

She prepared a lavish feast in honor of the man who had master-minded the extinction of her people, and had tricked the king into signing such an edict. Then, she revealed her true identity. She was a Jew! The king of Persia took pity on her because he loved her deeply. She saved her people, and did so with grace and class.

Ziven thought to herself, *"If there is ever a moment like that for me, I will not hesitate to take it and make it mine! I will do as Queen Esther did, and risk everything for that which is more important!"*

As for the days of Purim, first would be the fasting, then the feast. She only had to prepare for her ima, her aba, her husband, and herself, but it was always a lot of work. Everything had to be perfectly aligned with tradition. She had prepared for Purim so many times that she could do it with her eyes closed. *"Traditions are preserved to help us remember who we are and what God expects us to do. The problem is, I don't know who I am... and I certainly don't know what God expects me to do!"* Ziven thought to herself. She shook off the cloud of self-pity and depression that surely would have consumed her, and returned to the task at hand. Duty energized much of her actions these days; duty and tradition.

"Ziven, this food is delicious, as usual. You have such a way with hamantaschen" (traditional triangle-shaped fruit-filled pastries). Michael cleared his throat to make an announcement, not knowing how it would be received. Ziven watched him curiously as he obviously fought to gather courage to continue. "I have been asked to visit San Francisco...." There was silence at the table, so Michael straightened and forced himself to continue. "San Francisco... California... in the United States." He looked around to see what reaction that statement might have created. Sensing only that they were waiting to hear more, he mumbled. "There is a good chance my job will relocate there."

Now he looked more intently into the faces and eyes of his beloved family. Ziven's parents were well-stricken with age and would need care soon. He had not spoken with Ziven about her feelings, but then again, they hadn't talked about much over the past 10 years of their marriage anyway. He did his thing, and she did hers. He didn't like it, but that was just the way things were; and he had accepted it. Well, he had tried to accept it.

As he and Ziven caught each other's eyes from across the table, something made him think of the first time he met her.

It was not the best of circumstances. He had been injured while helping a neighbor repair shingles on his roof, when Michael's ladder leaned to the side and he fell 30 feet. He did not remember hitting the concrete. He only remembered waking up with the bright light of the sun shining in his face. Suddenly a face was near his, asking him to repeat his name. Beams of sunlight radiated around her head like a halo. Her image was shadowed, but he squinted and blinked until he could focus on her face. It was the most beautiful face he had ever seen!

Her long brown hair was pulled to the side and fell in a graceful flowing swoosh of color down her side. Her olive skin was clear and bright. Her eyes were a golden color, like a bald eagle, with little flecks of green and a dark circle of deep blue surrounding her pupils. They seemed to pierce him to his very soul. He was breathless, but he didn't know if it was from her beauty or from his injuries.

A far away musical voice was asking him if he were okay, but he was distracted and his mind was foggy. It took every energy to bring his mind to the present. Then, he realized that the voice he heard was not far away… it was from the angel of mercy who was helping him!

What is she asking me?" he wondered. "Oh, yea… my name… What IS my name?"

Then, he thought he might just stay there and look into her beautiful eyes. He had never seen such stunningly beautiful eyes before.

"You're just fine!" Ziven laughed as she pushed him away and got up, her shiny hair flying as she spun around, and her blazing eyes teasing him.

This gave Michael an opportunity to see Ziven's long slender frame. Her shape was curvy and her movements graceful. Her sideways smile revealed a dimple in her cheek. That was the moment. The moment that he knew he wanted to spend the rest of his life with this fiery angel of mercy.

That was a long time ago," Michael sharply told himself. Then the smile faded from his face as he sighed and thought, *"Things change."*

He looked at his bride again. She was older, no longer the young girl he had met, but she was still very beautiful. Why had they drifted apart? Was there anything still between them? He wondered if it was too late for a life of happiness together. Maybe this is just what they needed; a change of scenery and routine. His mind was made up that if Ziven chose to stay in Jerusalem, he would leave her. Of course, he would give her a "Writing of Divorcement," but if she chose to join him in the United States, he would give their marriage a try again. He would give it every effort possible. This would be her choice. He was being more than fair. It was now, or never!

For a moment, Ziven thought she could hear Michael's thoughts. But, as she tried to focus on them, they eluded her. It was as though she was not permitted to communicate as freely with people as she could with all other living things. That thought made her feel lonely. She could sometimes see their auras, (a bright glowing light outlining all living creatures) but could only rarely feel their thoughts.

For just a moment, she let her mind return to the day she first saw Michael. He had been helping a neighbor replace shingles and was goofing around. He certainly was not being careful. She remembered seeing him fall in slow motion. Even now it was painful to rehearse it in her mind. Then, there was that sound! That horrible sound of his body hitting the concrete! How could anyone survive after making that sound?

She rushed to his side and checked his vitals. She put her ear to his chest... Yes, there was a heartbeat! Then, she put her cheek to his face and could feel his breath. He was alive! *"Thank GOD he is alive!"* she had shouted within herself.

Ziven tried to wake him without moving him in case he was injured seriously. She asked him again and again if he were okay, and what his name was. She saw him open his dark brown eyes, blink a few times, and then he just started staring into her hazel eyes. There was an awkward moment when she thought he was going to try to kiss her...

So, she did what she always did… she pushed him away. She never let anyone inside of her protective shell.

She looked at Michael now. He looked so very tired. It was as though life had worn him down and there was no longer any life or light in him. Certainly, there was no light in his eyes…. at least not when he looked at her. It was a miracle that she was expecting a child. She had done her duty as usual, but didn't feel anything. She didn't feel love. She didn't feel appreciated. She certainly didn't feel cherished. She sighed and could only feel loneliness, but today she felt even more lonely than usual.

Before they could continue the discussion about a possible move to the United States, and what that would mean for their family, there was a large crashing sound… and that's the last thing Ziven remembered.

Chapter IV
Two Hours Earlier

Hashim's mind was laser focused on the task at hand. His instructions were clear: "Calmly walk into the lobby, enter the restroom, leave the backpack full of explosives in the garbage can, and return to the van within 30 seconds. If something goes wrong, shout a praise to Allah, wait for the bomb to go off, and meet your glorious destiny."

Hashim is an Arabic name that means, "One who destroys evil." This is certainly what they were going to do today.

Ehud Barak, the newly elected Prime Minister of Jerusalem, was known for his big talk about forming a coalition with the Centre Party, the left-wing Meretz, Yisrael BaAliya, the religious Shaws, and the National Religious Party. He was also known for ignoring all Jewish holidays, and holding his own lavish parties and feasts to honor himself in direct conflict with these festivals. Purim was no exception.

Barak was just about to begin the parade and procession toward the West Jaffa Gate just as the Holy Shabbat was beginning. This pageantry was to end at the Khan Theatre where a special theatrical production was to be made in his honor that evening. Barak was just about to leave his hotel in Jerusalem near the border of the Christian and the Jewish Quarters.

Hashim was not given this name at birth, he was given it when he joined the Sayyid Qutab and adopted the Manichean view of the world. Now, his birth family doesn't exist, only The Brotherhood. These are the ones who truly understand him. These are the only people who care about him.

He looked around him as his "brothers" were putting on their backpacks in the dark van with no windows. They had each been given new names as well when they joined up.

Amir was tall and slender with clear skin and a regal air about him. He was well named since "Amir" means "Prince." Everyone seemed to follow him and he led effortlessly. He never seemed to show any sign of nervousness or fear.

Asad was shorter and a bit stocky. He had a hot temper and his eyes always seemed to flash quickly with anger whenever talking about the injustices of the bureaucracy of leadership in Israel. "Asad" means "Lion" in Arabic. He, too, was well named.

"Hakeem" means "wise." Hakeem had a slight build, wore black glasses that were far too loose, and usually averted his eyes. It was Hakeem that figured out Barak's next location. He was instrumental in the success of this mission. As the van turned a corner and began to slow, Hashim's heart began to race. *"Now is my moment in history! Now is the time! Someone must stand up against evil!"* he thought to himself. He looked at his "brothers" and they were thinking the same thing.

The white van stopped, and the side door opened. The four young boys poured out of the van and took off in different directions. Hashim walked straight to the front doors of the most expensive hotel in Jerusalem, the Mamilla Hotel on Shlomo ha-Melekh street.

Hashim could see Hakeem out of the corner of his eye, but this was a time to focus. He could not think about the people who would be hurt. He could not think about his father's face if he knew what had become of his son. He could not think of his mother. "Focus!"

Hashim, stiff as a board, walked straight to the men's room on the main floor, dropped his backpack into the trash receptacle, and began making his way back to the front glass doors. He could hear a shout in the neighboring building...

"Allahu Akbar!"

Everyone in the lobby heard it as well. Suddenly, it seemed as though everyone were looking at Hashim. The frightened look on his face may have given it away, but the security guards near the front door were certainly heading slowly toward him.

He panicked and began running toward the street and cried, "Allahu Akbar!" (God is greater!)

Hashim never made it to the street. He never even made it out of the lobby.

Chapter V
The Explosion

Ziven's eye lids were too heavy to open. She felt as though her body were 10 times larger than normal. It was an expansiveness that she recognized, so she relaxed and let herself feel the sensation. Her soul seemed to grow larger and larger until it filled the area the size of a city block. A by-product of this phenomenon was that she would know and understand every molecule of every portion of space within that area. It was an amazing concept that she had learned to control... at least for a short while.

She could see every ant, every particle of food or dust, every creature or human being and what they were doing or thinking. It was a fetal version of omnipresence that was stunningly easy to understand and very difficult to maintain. The sensation left her appreciating how it must be for JEHOVAH, the Great God of all. (Although it was contrary to Jewish teachings, she felt inside that He knew her individually and personally. This gave her great comfort and eased some of her loneliness.) This time, however, she wondered if it was a dream because something was different. She felt as though she were somehow "disconnected" from reality. If she were dreaming, why couldn't she wake up? She had to try. It took every energy within her, focused energy... until finally she could feel herself being pulled back into the harsh consciousness of reality.

Ziven strained to open her eyes, but the deepness of her sleep was like a wet blanket... heavy and clinging. Something was wrong. Something was terribly wrong! She was having difficulty breathing. There was a strange pressure on her chest, concentrated and dense. She tried to get up, but seemed to be pinned down. Then, she realized that she indeed was pinned down under a solid mass of concrete. For the first time in her life, Ziven felt panic.

She didn't know if the darkness was because of the hour, or the dust in the air. There certainly was a lot of dust in the air! It made breathing almost impossible... or was that the effect of being pinned underneath the rubble of a collapsed building? That had to be it! But how did this happen? Who is responsible? Why did this happen to her and her family?

Suddenly, she was keenly aware of her surroundings and began to try to call out for her ima and her aba with short painful breaths. "Michael!" He would help her, she thought to herself! Then, in an abrupt alarm she wondered, *"Where is Michael?!"*

Ziven began to take a personal inventory of her body. Her head was aching as though an explosion were still going on inside. She could feel warm, wetness on the right side of her face. "Head wounds bleed a lot," she told herself. "Nothing to worry about."

Her right eye was swollen shut, but she could slightly open her left eye. Blackness. No help there.

She could not feel her legs. Perhaps that was a good thing. Her right arm was pinned underneath her body, but she thought she might be able to move her left arm a little bit. Sure enough, she was able to wriggle it a little bit. This gave her hope that she could eventually free herself. Even if it were a very slight hope... it was something to hold on to.

Ziven woke up with a start. She must have passed out. It was morning now, and nothing had changed. She had hoped it had been a terrible nightmare, but it wasn't.

"Michael?"

"Ima?"

"Aba?"

Ziven called out. Nothing.

Then, she thought she saw some movement out of the corner of her eye... her one good eye. "Michael? Is that you?" She heard a moan. It was Michael.

Then, she heard her Aba's voice, sweet, penetrating, and crystal clear. "Ziven, you will be alright. Everything is going to be alright. Help is on the way." That was strange... She didn't exactly "hear" her aba's voice... it was more like she "felt" it. It was like when she would communicate with the plants or animals. The words just sort of sank into her heart and her mind translated the words for her.

Ziven heard Michael moan again. "Michael... Michael, are you okay?"

"Ziven?"

"I am here."

"I... I cannot move."

She answered, "I am trapped as well, but help is on the way."

Ziven felt a strange chill go through her body the moment she spoke those words. She knew they were true. She didn't know how, but she knew it. Then, her mind slowly floated away from full consciousness, drawn like wet clay pulls each step downward with a strong and steady force.

Chapter VI
Butterflies

Ashes were raining down in graceful flutters, covering the debris with a fresh coat of white, like newly fallen snow. A deafening silence was in the air. All time seemed to stop as the shock of what had just happened began to sink in.

Joshua had been daydreaming as he walked slowly home along the edge of the Christian Quarter toward the West Gate. He hadn't noticed the pleasant weather, the sounds of children laughing, nor the chirping of springtime birds. He had been too distracted by his own thoughts. Thoughts of his only son lying in a hospital bed. The doctors said he had fainted because his blood was weak.

He had just left the side of his five-year-old son, Jacob, and things didn't look good. He hadn't even noticed the white van speeding off even though it had almost hit him. Joshua was making his way home to discuss medical options with his wife and thinking about how he was going to come up with the money for medical bills when he was knocked off his feet by the blast. It hit his side like a wave of concrete and sent him sprawling through the air, landing in the street 35 feet away.

Joshua didn't know how much time had passed, but he knew that he had been unconscious. When he woke up, his face was covered with dust and he had to dig at his eyes to get them clear enough to take a look around him. His mind was reeling, and everything seemed to be moving in slow motion. Desperately grasping for straws of reality, Joshua tried to get to his feet, but his mind didn't seem to be connected to his legs. "My head HURTS!" he muttered to himself as he tried again to rise. He closed his eyes, and took a slow deep breath. This only caused him to cough robustly until his lungs burned and his ribs shot stinging pain through his chest.

Holding his side seemed to help what surely were bruised ribs, if not broken ones. As he staggered to his feet, he surveyed his surroundings. *"What happened?"* he incredulously asked himself. He could hardly recognize anything around him. People were milling about in a daze. The rubble of concrete and twisted metal was everywhere. Crying children could be heard in the distance, and faint sirens as well.

"There are survivors buried here! They await your rescue."

Joshua spun around to see who had spoken to him, but no one was nearby. He longed to go home and make sure his wife was alright. He ached to return to the hospital to see his son. But it was as though he were caught in the current of a rushing river. He could not leave, no matter how desperately he wanted to, nor how badly he was hurting. He knew he needed to start digging. Somehow, he knew that if he did not do this, people would die.

Elijah didn't hear the blast. Elijah had not heard anything since he was very little when a very hot fever and lots of little red dots had covered his body as a six-year-old child. He didn't hear it, but he did *feel* it!

As a deaf-mute, there was little Elijah could do to support himself. The easiest path would have been to join the many beggars that hold their cups out for passers-by to contribute to, but Elijah did not want to do that. He found that he liked to carve wood, and that he had a particular gift for it. Selling practical things to locals brought him enough money for his rent, but it was the tourists that purchased his most precious items, and these brought him enough money for food and clothing.

He loved to make Olive Wood Nativity sets, and imagined himself visiting the Christ Child at His birth. It was not difficult to learn about Jesus. All one had to do was to follow the tourists. A warm feeling of hope and light seemed to fill his heart the moment he first comprehended that because of the Messiah, he would someday hear again, and that he was known by God and loved by Him.

Elijah was near the Christian Quarter preparing to close his stand for the evening when it happened. A sudden gust of powerfully tangible wind, as solid as a wall, slammed into him. Startled, he seemed to remember flying through the air in slow motion and seeing everyone and everything else down the narrow corridor blown over at once. Things were flying through the dusty air in one great billowing surge; bits and pieces of concrete, glass, etc.

The sun was beginning to lower in the sky, but it seemed much darker; far too dark to see clearly. As Elijah made his way to a clearing, he climbed over a pile of rubble to see only more piles of rubble!

"What could have caused this?" he wondered.

He felt something soft below his feet, and looked down, then jumped backward, almost falling as he did so. Blinking his eyes in unbelief, he bent down to touch the red item, but stopped just short of reaching it. Could it actually be? No! He held his lurching stomach and looked away, closing his eyes tightly.

Elijah took a moment, gathered his courage, and then looked at the disconnected hand of a child that he had stepped on. As he looked more closely, there were many similar remains littering the entire area. Tears welled up in Elijah's eyes as he stumbled forward in no particular direction at all.

Then he heard it.

Well, he didn't actually "hear" it... or did he? It was more like a feeling. Something drew his attention to a specific mound where a man was spinning around like a mad man looking for something.

"There are survivors buried here! They await your rescue."

Elijah immediately understood and began to dig. Joshua said nothing and began to do the same. They worked side-by-side for hours under a full moon. Heaving large rocks with their bloodied hands, coughing up black ash, and pushing themselves past exhaustion, Joshua and Elijah didn't dare stop. They knew that if they stopped to rest, they might not be able to find the strength to start again. They also knew that somewhere deep below, were people who were waiting, counting on them to get them out.

Emergency vehicles came and went. Other men joined the search for the living, but mostly found the dead... and pieces of the dead! An old woman brought the volunteers some fresh water. Eventually, the sun started to illuminate the horrific scene. Four city blocks were gone. Vanished! No professional mourners were needed here. Sobbing women and children were everywhere.

The fires were mostly out now, but smoke and dust still filled the air. Amid the horror of the task, there was a moment of surreal beauty that caused time to stand still.

Suddenly, a kaleidoscope of Monarch butterflies emerged from the debris. They were everywhere! Everyone stopped digging, stopped searching, stopped moving. After an audible gasp, there was silence as everyone simply watched the cloud of butterflies swarm and flutter, and slowly rise into the heavens.

No one moved for the longest time. It seemed to be a message from the Universe; a reminder that even in the midst of something as horrifying as this, life goes on. Somehow, it finds a way to continue.

Then, the noise of everyone reacting to what they had just seen began to rise. Suddenly, Joshua thought he heard something to his right. Or, could he have imagined it? "Quiet everyone!" he shouted!

Elijah saw his gesture and held still as a statue. Quickly, Joshua began digging with more energy and fervor than ever before. "There's someone down here!" he shouted.

<hr>

For one brief moment, Ziven opened her eyes. The faces of everyone she could see were covered with a mask of white powder, leaving only two eye-holes, small nostril-vents, and a large smiling row of teeth for a mouth. It was as though everyone had been swimming in fine white pastry sugar or baking flour.

"What happened?" she asked herself. Ziven's home was gone. The entire area was flattened. She barely recognized the neighborhood she grew up in. Trees were shouting screams of pain and agony as they burned in raging flames. Then, things went black again. Suddenly everything was very dark and very quiet.

The next thing Ziven knew, she was lying in a bed with side rails. It was not a comfortable bed. She knew instantly that it was a hospital bed and that it was Michael she could hear breathing heavily from another bed nearby.

The scratchy, stiff, white sheets were stained with drops of blood from a previous patient. She wondered if she would survive the care, but looked at the tired eyes of nurses darting about and decided to have compassion on them. They were doing the best they could. They must have families too... families that were affected by the many years of war and tumult. Surely, she would be alright in their care. She kept repeating this mantra to herself, only half believing it.

Then her eyes caught hold of movement nearby. She watched morbidly as a large air bubble made its way up the tube and into her arm where the IV was pumping fluids and medications into her body. *"I wonder if that is enough air to cause a heart attack. This is not the way I would have chosen to die... but if it is my time, I am ready,"* she thought to herself as she forced her body to relax and took a deep breath.

Her mind began to wander. She never did see Ima, nor Aba... but she was told they hadn't survived. *"I must be in shock, because I feel numb,"* she thought to herself. *"Shouldn't I be crying? Shouldn't I be sad? I don't feel anything. Why don't I feel anything?!! What's wrong with me?"*

Ziven looked over at Michael. He looked like he had been through a meat grinder. White gauze bandages with large areas of red or deep reddish-brown seemed to cover his entire body. He was sleeping. That was a good thing. She could hear the deep heaviness of his breathing along with the beeping of machines. Tubes were tying him to the machines; obviously keeping him under close surveillance. Then, she became aware of her own appearance. Much the same.

"Oh, Aba! Oh, Ima! What will I ever do without you?" She felt her heart sink at the thought.

Ziven let her mind wander to happier days. She could see her ima in the kitchen preparing for a Holy Shabbat. Her long ebony hair, pulled back in a bun as she carefully prepared the challah (braided bread) with sesame seeds, Matzah balls, lamb stew, stuffed dates, and Rugelach cookies with extra chocolate... just like she liked them. Everything was done with such love and care. Each bite of delicious food translated into the consequence of profound love as it melted in your mouth.

Her mother was cheerfully round, but not without sorrows. There were moments when Ziven would catch her "ima" unaware and see a deep furrow on her brow as she was thinking of something too personal to ever speak about... some secret heartbreak... some private sorrow that her mind had momentarily travelled to. Now that secret is buried under tons of rubble. Now Ziven would never have an opportunity to ask her about it.

Then, there was her aba. He was not one to ever reveal his humanness. Impatience and the perpetual infallibility of his opinion defined his character. Culturally, he had learned how to argue points of the Torah. He was the victorious winner of every discussion without fail... and he never let you forget that fact.

He had a way of stroking his long grey beard and looking right through a person. This would unsettle them enough that he could attack the heart of the matter with logic. He truly loved the never-ending discussions about doctrinal points, interpretations, and hypotheses. Ziven wondered if there would be never-ending discussions in heaven. If not, she didn't think her aba would be very happy there.

The fogginess of her mind was starting to lift now, and Ziven was left to feel the depth of the reality of what had happened.

"Oh, Aba! Oh, Ima! What will I ever do without you? Now there is only me and Michael... and..." (she gasped) *"THE BABY!"*

A sudden panic enveloped her. She pushed the nurse's button at the side of her bed and waited to ask the question, "Is my baby alright?" Then, unable to do anything else... Ziven began to cry uncontrollably, her body convulsing with sobbing waves of worry and despair.

Despite the overwhelming fear of what she might find, she slowly forced her hands to her abdomen...

Chapter VII
Two Months Later

The flight from Tel Aviv to San Francisco, CA was a long 23-hour one. Michael was deeply involved with some books. He was always involved with some books. Ziven sighed, and tried to look on the positive side. San Francisco is another world; an adventure. She tried to stir up in her heart an excitement and a romance about the move.

She was fluent in English, so that wouldn't be a problem. She had secretly studied it and was so proud that she could both speak and read English quite well. Language seemed to come easily for her. Ima had told her once that it was a special gift from JEHOVAH, and that she had been given special gifts with the task of using them to help God bless the lives of others. She wondered how a gift of learning languages could be helpful to anyone else.

There is a lot to see in San Francisco, so she should not get bored too easily. And, it was a city of romance... at least that is what all the books she had read seemed to portray. Perhaps Michael would look at her and actually SEE her. Maybe she would no longer be invisible. She could feel a hope welling up from somewhere inside of her.

She looked over at Michael and tried to see into his soul. She could see his aura, and it was greener than usual. Perhaps he was just tired.

Ziven was tired too. She was tired of being overlooked and ignored. She was tired of being misunderstood and unappreciated. She was tired of being diminished and dismissed. Yes, she was very tired. So very tired...

Then, as it often did subconsciously, her hand made its way to her swollen abdomen. She is 6 months pregnant now. This was the farthest along her physician would allow her to fly, so it was actually perfect timing. Her wounds from being trapped under a collapsed building were mostly healed now. It was lucky for her that the baby was not injured during that terrible experience. Everything seemed to check out alright with the physician prior to the transfer.

Things just seemed to fall into place for this move. Maybe it really will make a difference. Maybe she and Michael can have a new and beautiful life together after all. Maybe...

She looked over at Michael and tried to summon feelings of love for him, but it made her even wearier. His name, "Michael" is Hebrew for one who is "like God." Certainly he had it in him. After all, Ziven fell in love with him, didn't she? She began to list the things she loved about him in her journal:

1. When he smiles, his face lights up like the sunshine.
2. His heart is so kind towards little children, and they truly adore him.
3. He serves strangers without giving it a second thought.
4. There is no one better at thinking of solutions to issues.
5. He is so incredibly intelligent.
6. He is so creative when it comes to ways to use technology to resolve problems.
7. His talent with sketching is stunning. I love it when he draws life from his perspective.
8. He is my husband, and I have made covenants before God to give myself to him.
9. He is the father of our child. He will be a good father.
10. Somewhere in his heart, deep down, he must feel some love for me. He used to anyway.

As she pondered these things, a thought came into her mind. "This is according to plan. Everything will be alright." These words penetrated her soul and she knew they were true. Somehow, she wasn't sure how, but she knew they were true, and she was comforted.

Since she was making lists, Ziven used the rest of the time on the airplane to plan out all the things she needed to do to settle in to the new place and find an apartment. There was so much to do, and it would fall to her since Michael would be busy at his new job.

Then, there was the list of things she would like to see in the San Francisco area; places she had read about in books -- "touristy" things like riding a trolley car, seeing the famous Golden Gate Bridge, the crooked Lombard Street, and Alcatraz Island. She was especially intrigued with the Redwood Forest. "I wonder what those old trees will have to say. Will they be different than the ancient olive trees? Will I be able to feel them or communicate with them at all?"

She had studied the Internet about Alcatraz Island and was surprised to learn that it had been much more than a prison (like it had been portrayed in an American movie she had heard about).

* 1775 discovered and mapped by Spanish explorer Juan Manuel de Ayala. Named "La Isla de los Alcatraces" because of all of the Pelicans.

* 1850 became a military fortress with 100 cannons to protect San Francisco Bay. First West Coast lighthouse. Used as a military prison.

* 1861 it became a prison for Confederate sympathizers during the American Civil War and citizens accused of treason.

* 1885 added Native American Indians who were labeled "rebellious" during the land disagreements with the federal government.

* 1889 added inmates who opposed the Spanish-American War.

* 1912 inmates finished building the largest reinforced concrete building with 600 cells, a hospital, mess hall, and other prison buildings.

* 1934 it became a maximum-security facility run by the U.S. Justice Department.

* 1963 closed due to high expense of management.

* 1969 Native Americans claimed the island and hoped to establish a university and museum on the island.

* 1971 Native Americans were removed by the U.S. President Richard Nixon and sent to reservations, or specific lands that they were not allowed to leave.

* 1972 became a tourist site. Today over 1 million tourists visit it each year.

Ziven was intrigued to learn about the Native American involvement with the island. She had been reading books about Native Americans since she was old enough to read English. She had learned about the Plains Indians, the 5 Civilized Tribes, Woodland Tribes, Great Basin Tribes, Southwestern Tribes, and others. Her favorite, of course, were the Cherokee people. Her heart stirred within her each time she learned more about them.

"Perhaps I will have access to more information about my people now that we will be living in America," she thought.

"MY PEOPLE..."

The thought felt as though she were surrounded by a warm blanket, comfortable and peaceful. Still, it was interesting to her that blood could be such a deciding factor in the identity of a person; even greater than one's upbringing. She would have to think about that some more another time.

She had been raised to respect her elders, to respect traditions, and to respect people in general. She had been taught to never fail in doing her "duty" no matter what the cost. Her aba had taught her to respect learning and education.

Innate to her soul was also a deep respect for nature, and spiritual abilities that seemed unique to her alone. She relished her peculiarities and was anxious to explore them in this new chapter of her life.

Michael looked up and asked, "Whatcha workin' on?" Ziven smiled at the attempted "American" accent. She answered, "I'm just making lists. You know how I am."

"How are you feeling?" he looked down at her swollen abdomen tied down with a seat belt and shifted her weight uncomfortably. "I'm okay." She sighed. "Thanks." This was the first time she could remember him asking about her health. Surely, he had asked her before... but she could not remember it. Even after the bombing that had killed her parents, and put them both in the hospital for a month, he didn't seem to notice her. She felt virtually invisible most of the time.

Ziven chased the negative thought path from her mind. It only made her feel lonelier and would lead to self-pity and negative thoughts. She didn't like to think of herself as a negative person. She was constantly assuming the best of people, driving any negative thoughts from her mind, and had trained her outlook to be optimistic. How could Michael think she was a negative person? How could anyone believe that about her? She was at a total loss and caught off guard every time he accused her of that.

Was Ziven simply out of touch with reality as Michael had repeatedly described her? *"Anything is possible,"* she told herself. *"I know I'm not perfect, no one is. I guess I need to take a closer look at myself and see if there is any truth to that so I can change. I love Michael and want to have a happy marriage with him. With this little girl on the way, she deserves that. Besides, Michael had asked about how I am feeling... that is a good sign, isn't it?"*

He was making an effort, and she appreciated it. Ziven looked over at Michael and smiled weakly, but he didn't notice. He was already deeply absorbed in his book. The short-lived attention would need to be attended to more quickly next time. Opportunities are rare and need to be acknowledged and maximized or they will never increase in frequency. She scolded herself for not being a better wife and companion.

Michael was not merely her only family. She was his as well. She began to wonder if he ever felt as lonely as she did. The truth was, he did;

but he didn't trust his feelings to his wife. He didn't trust sharing them with anyone.

<hr>

Michael had been raised as an only child, but he did have siblings. He was the youngest of three children, and the only boy. His father never had good health and always seemed frailer than his age. His mother and sisters were cold and distant toward him. He often felt invisible, and he liked it that way. He would create his own imaginary world and entertain himself. He learned to inventively find solutions to problems, resourcefully figure out ways to educate himself and to soothe the deep empty sorrow that grew within him each day in his loneliness.

Michael drove himself to excel in his studies in an attempt to get attention from his parents. But, by the time Michael was old enough to select what kind of school to go to, his father was already 65 years old and seemed completely inaccessible.

It's not that his parents didn't love him. They were just consumed with their own worries. It's not that his sisters Rina and Nadar didn't care about him, it's just that they were simply unaware of his sorrowful existence in their midst. As Michael attempted to reach out to express his feelings, he would be dismissed immediately. It didn't take long before he simply stopped trying.

In Yerushalayim Torah Academy for Boys, Michael began acting out. Subconsciously, he hoped to be noticed by his father, but it was always his mother that showed up whenever he was in trouble. This was humiliating because the other boys began to call him a "tziflon" which essentially means, "Mama's Boy"... a name he could not tolerate.

Each torturous day of being taunted and teased by the other boys found Michael exploding in anger and fist fights. Eventually, a hard outer-crust grew around him until only a "tough guy" persona could be seen.

One day as he was walking home after a particularly difficult day, he heard a moan from a side alley-way. It was the merchant who owned the bookstore Michael liked to frequent.

Michael ran to his side, carefully looking around for any remaining assailants and propped up the head of his friend. He had obviously been stabbed in the stomach because he was holding his belly and was covered with deep red blood; lots of it. Michael didn't know what to do. Should he cry out for help? Should he leave this man to go find help? Was it too late? The old man looked weakly into Michael's eyes, and with labored breathing took one deep rumbly breath; then exhaled for what seemed to be an eternity. That was it. His head suddenly became very heavy on Michael's young lap and his eyes closed.

Something inside of Michael broke that day, and he felt a most profound despair. As he numbly made his way home that day, he arrived at an empty house. Not truly aware of his surroundings, he sat down on a chair in the middle of the room and just stared into space.

He didn't know how long he had been sitting there, and he didn't realize that his clothes were covered with blood. The sun had gone down long ago, as Michael sat in the darkness. As his mother and sisters entered the darkened room, lit a kerosene lamp on the table, and sat impassively around the table—Michael hardly noticed. In what seemed to be an eternity of silence, they sat. No one said a word.

The minutes and hours ticked on through the night, but no one moved a muscle. Only the occasional sniff of one of his sisters could be heard. At some point, Michael realized that he should probably ask about what was upsetting his sisters and mother. But, it was just easier to sit in silence.

The following days were filled with preparations, but not many words. Michael's father had died of a heart attack at the very moment Michael was in that horrible alley way watching his friend take his last breath. Now, his mother and sisters were moving closer to family, but he would not be going with them.

Against Jewish tradition, he would not be taking care of his family, but Michael didn't care. He didn't feel sorry. He didn't feel anything. He had chosen to turn off all emotion. That was the only way he could cope. Feel nothing; that was the plan.

36

Michael was not surprised when his mother didn't seem to care whether he moved with them or not. She had said, "You are 16. Do what you want."

The streets were not kind to Michael and it was a difficult life. He didn't let anyone get close to him, not really. Not until the day he met Ziven.

In the airplane, Ziven lets her mind imagine what their little girl might look like, and how her life will be very different from that of her mother. Schools... a land of opportunity... Ziven smiled and drifted off to sleep.

Her rest was short lived as a barely understandable loud voice said over the speakers, "Please return to your seats and adhere to the buckle-up sign. We are experiencing some engine trouble, but there is no need to worry." Something about the looks on the faces of the flight attendants told Ziven that there really WAS reason to worry. She fought back feelings of uneasiness and looked at Michael with could easily be described as a silent shout of regret:

"Why didn't I pay attention to the instructions at the beginning of the flight about what to do during an emergency?! There was something about a flotation device and some kind of oxygen masks that come from the ceiling..."

Ziven looked out the window and saw sparks and smoke coming from one of the engines! The cabin was bouncing around. People were unsuccessfully holding back panic. Some were sobbing. Everyone was afraid. Everyone but Ziven. She just felt sick.

Michael took Ziven's hand, and with a rare expression of true compassion said, "Everything is going to be alright." She melted as she gazed into his deep brown eyes and wanted so badly to believe him that she forced herself to do so whole-heartedly.

Michael looked at Ziven. *"She is truly beautiful. She is good and kind. Why does she always put me down? Why is she always so negative? Doesn't she know that I want to have a loving relationship with her? We just never seem to be able to talk to each other without pain. I don't know how much longer I can do this...*

"Could it possibly be me? What if I'm the one who is sabotaging our relationship? Is it possible that I am misunderstanding everything she says and seeing it as negative? If that is true, why? I can see that it is hurting her. That's not what I want... not really. I guess I just never learned how to be truly caring. Ziven deserves to be treated like a queen. She deserves someone who would truly love her and blossom with her into a long happy life together. I don't know how to stop this vicious cycle.

"And our daughter... she is carrying our daughter." Michael sighed. *"I love my daughter already... why can't I love her mother completely? Is something wrong with me? I know I am prideful and impatient... Maybe this new change will be just what we need. A change of scenery, a change of heart...*

"I hope we make it through this so I can try again. Everything truly will be alright." Michael tried to comfort himself.

It seemed like an eternity, but the plane finally stopped safely on the runway in San Francisco.

Tears of relief flooded from Ziven's eyes. Michael didn't understand why she would be crying after everything proved to be alright, but that was okay... he didn't need to. Maybe it was hormones. It didn't matter, though; Ziven simply wanted his comfort when she cried. That's all she needed from him. Perhaps someday he would understand.

It was a long two hours waiting in lines and going through customs, and Ziven was exhausted after the long emotional flight. The balancing act that it is to stand with an additional 20 pounds of stomach leaning forward wreaks havoc on the lower back. "Why don't they offer chairs for people who wait in long lines? Surely I am not the first to be terribly uncomfortable." She thought to herself, then she sighed. It is always easy to be negative when one is tired, hungry or uncomfortable... but her ima had always taught her that the easy path is not always the best path. "One must choose to act, rather than to be acted upon." She would always say. Suddenly startled, Ziven had let the line move forward a few feet. She moved forward feeling like insignificant sheep being herded mindlessly to a sheering. Then, she forced herself to look forward. After all, it was a bright future; a new place, a new life, an adventure.

These thoughts lifted Ziven's spirits, and she smiled. Michael was looking at her. He didn't do that often, but this time he did... and her smile reminded him that he loved her... deep down he still loved her.

Chapter VIII
San Francisco

The next few days were full of the busy-ness of looking for an apartment, finding a new doctor to deliver the baby, a nearby synagogue, places to get kosher groceries, Michael's new offices, a library full of delicious books, and learning how to use the BART transportation system. Once they were settled in, and their few belongings unpacked and organized, Ziven loved wandering around the streets of San Francisco. She never had a plan, she just liked to take it all in and wander wherever her feet would take her.

Fisherman's Wharf was a plethora of sights, sounds, and smells. The salty ocean air floated on a gentle breeze that was just enough to blow away the morning mist that clung to the earth and plants all around her. She faced the direction of the wind and let her long light brown hair flow behind her.

As she breathed in the salty air, she was aware of other smells as well. Fresh sourdough bread, something that was fried in grease, and fish... yes, lots of different fish smells!

Ziven walked to the end of the pier and looked down at the greenish water. To her surprise and delight, she saw dozens of sea lions floating on their backs, arm in arm and quite asleep. Occasionally one of them would move, so she understood that they were alive, but resting. The cute whiskers and sleek dark and shiny bodies were very endearing. Sea gulls called and cried all around her. They seemed to have no fear of humans... in fact, they seemed to be waiting for bread crumbs or other food to be left behind. She wondered if they had forgotten how to fish, and if the presence of humans had changed their entire ecosystem for generations to come.

Ziven made her way to the seashore... took off her shoes... and walked into the water. The waves were surprisingly warm and bubbly. The smell of salt seemed to explode from the foamy bubbles as they crashed upon the sandy beach. She could feel the sand beneath her feet erode as the water receded. Little bubbles and holes remained in the sand as the only evidence that little sand crabs were scurrying down deeper after each wave of water had forced them to float to the surface.

Looking out at the horizon, where the sky seemed to touch the edge of the water... Ziven felt part of the entire world all at once. It was a beautiful feeling! She could imagine the billions of creatures in the sea, living and dying at that very moment! Large creatures like the blue whale or the giant squid, sharks, manta rays, sea turtles... and small creatures like protozoa, krill, seahorses, anemones, and coral. All part of the same ocean. All part of the ocean she had joined at that very moment!

Suddenly, she didn't have to imagine anything. She instantly became conscious of every living creature in the waters of the earth. She could sense their thoughts, their joys, their struggles, their lives. It was exhilarating.

She thought of the land she stood upon, also part of the whole, and all life living on it. She thought of the cycle of life-giving water that started with beautiful thunder storms drenching the earth, and then eventually flowing back to the ocean after giving so much light and life along the way. Complete comprehension and profound respect flowed into her at the same time. She took a deep breath to totally relax and expand her ability to feel it all at once.

Ziven could suddenly feel the energy and life in the water as it lapped gently at her feet. It was like little glowing particles of life entering her body and infusing her soul with joy. She felt the urge to praise God. She felt the urge to sing within her soul a song of praise to the creator of all things. It was an overwhelming distillation of pure delight. She felt the child within her leap and dance! It startled her because she was so immersed in the sensations her soul had been experiencing, that she had almost forgotten that she was not alone.

At that moment, she could sense the personality of her daughter. It was only a split second, but in that instant, her baby's personality was communicated to her as a bubbly, dancing soul, full of sweet bliss, a kindness and gentleness that could only come from a "child of God."

As she stood there on the beach, Ziven pondered upon that thought... that her daughter was a *child of God.*" The thought *"Truth"* seemed to drench the molecules of her very being... from her head down to her toes and beyond. It was like a warm tingly feeling that left an imprint of profound safety and love.

That was an interesting sensation; similar to the time she heard her aba while she was trapped underneath the rubble of a collapsed building, but stronger than anything she had ever felt before. This was certainly something worthy of more thought and pondering. Ziven pushed the experience aside for the time being. It was time to return home. Michael would be home soon, and she had dinner to prepare.

Michael's first day at work was a blur. It was like drinking from a fire hose as he was trying to assimilate all of the new information and requirements... all in English. His mind seemed to lag behind just a little bit as he processed things he heard from English to Hebrew, and then back to English again so he could respond. It made his mind feel numb by the end of the day.

He was exhausted, but dreaded going home to rest... Ziven would
be there, and she would want to talk. He hated that. If he didn't talk to
her, she would be hurt... and he didn't want that. If he did talk to her, she
would want to talk more... and all he wanted to do was to relax! Talking
was too much work, especially after a hard day.

"Does this mean that I am a bad husband? Why is it so hard?"
Michael was grateful for the long train ride and the 10-minute walk home.
It would give him time to think and unwind before having to face her.

Michael took a deep breath and braced himself as he opened the
door to their stucco and brick home. They had been fortunate enough to
find a little house to rent in a fairly nice neighborhood. The walkway to
the front door was lined with rose bushes that seemed to fill the air with
a sweet aroma. It was difficult to remain in a grouchy mood after inhaling
such fragrant beauty. Somehow, life seemed better... more serene.

The smooth white walls, adobe shingles, with brick lined windows
was similar to their home in Jerusalem. Perhaps this is why they jumped at
the opportunity to lease it. There was even a small fenced back yard with
a large lemon tree that was heavily laden with little green balls that would
eventually brighten into lovely yellow lemons.

Ziven had a lot of plans for decorating their new home. She
seemed fulfilled and excited with new energy and purpose as she described
her plans for curtains, pillows, and rugs she would make. Michael liked
to see her this way. When she smiled, something inside of him sparked
feelings of love for her.... but it was like a faint memory, not a current call
to action.

Michael had determined to try to access those feelings of love for
her. He knew he needed to make a greater effort and not focus on his own
selfish desires as much. He just didn't know how to do it... or even what to
do. Perhaps all those years living on the streets in Jerusalem had left him
more scarred than he could recover from.

"Why isn't there some sort of checklist that I can just follow to make everything better? I'm just too tired to think about this right now." As Michael opened the door, he could smell something burning in the kitchen. He went to the stove and saw a pot with an explosion of eggs and egg shells in it. There was no water; it had been boiled away some time ago. There were yellow and white pieces of egg all over the ceiling, wall and floor.

"Where's Ziven?!!"

He turned off the stovetop and began to call her name, but there was no response. As Michael looked in each room, a panic began to swell within his heart and mind.

"Where is she? Something must be wrong!!"

His greatest fear was realized as he looked in the bathroom and saw Ziven lying face down on the floor. He heard a shriek scream her name that startled him; then he realized that the noise had come from his own mouth! He was truly terrified. She did not move.

"What is that number to dial in the United States when there is an emergency? They told me at work..."

Michael's mind was searching through the mountain of information he had received that day as he tried to revive his bride. Then, it was like a whisper to his mind... "Dial 9-1-1. Don't worry. Everything will be alright."

He suddenly felt calm. This surprised him. "I should be panicking... It feels wrong to be calm at a time like this."

He called 9-1-1 and they directed him about how to assess her condition. He was relieved to find out that she was breathing, but simply unconscious. It only took 3 minutes for the ambulance to arrive, but it seemed like the longest 3 minutes of his life!

The concerned and calming voice on the phone wanted to keep him on the phone, but he hung up. He wanted to focus on Ziven at that moment, and on nothing else. During that time, he stroked Ziven's long brown hair and talked to her.

He said things he would probably not have had the courage to say to her if she were conscious. "I love you so deeply! You are everything to me! I don't want to know what it is like to live life without you! You are the answer to all questions I have about myself, about life, about love, and about all things important. You are my reason for existing. I am utterly incomplete without you!"

He checked her pulse again... and it was soft and slow. Far too slow. Her eyes were rolled back and she was totally unresponsive. He began again...

"I need you to come back to me, Ziven! I need you! Our daughter needs you!..... I... love... you..."

The realization of these words sunk deep into Michael's heart as he admitted to himself that he truly did love her. Tears began to well up in his eyes; salty tears. The kind that burns the eyes but tastes good to the mouth.

He began to stroke her hair again, then realized that he had never touched her hair before. It was so soft and silky. Why had he never touched her hair? He looked at her limp hand in his. Her skin was so soft! Why had he never noticed this before? They had held hands many times, but he had never caressed her skin.

Michael felt a wave of guilt flood his weary mind as he realized that he had not been the best husband for this beautiful and amazing woman... and now... what if he didn't have an opportunity to make it up to her? What if this were the end?

Almost desperately and in a panic, he shook her shoulders, "Ziven! Ziven! Ziven!!" Then, he fell back and said under his breath, "I really do love you. Please don't leave me now... not before I have a chance to really be there for you."

Just at that moment, the Emergency Medical Technicians burst into the room and began quickly assessing Ziven's condition, and using their expertise to hook tubes and machines to her still body. Michael could only stay out of their way and silently pray.

He shouted silent prayers to the heavens. These were not ordinary prayers. No prayers like this could be sung while bobbing in front of the Wailing Wall of Jerusalem. This prayer was directly from his heart and soul. Nothing about it remotely resembled any of the Psalms or scriptures from the books of Moses.

"I need another chance! Please let her live, if only so I can live to make her happy! And our daughter, dear God... please let our daughter live also! I beg you for this blessing. I promise to be a better husband. I will change. I will not be so selfish. I will open my heart to my wife and to Thee, most Holy One. Oh, God of Abraham, Isaac, and Jacob... Creator of the heavens and earth... Father of miracles... I ask for another miracle today. Bring my Ziven back to me. Please, bring my Ziven back to me!"

<hr>

That night was the longest night of Michael's life. Every breath Ziven made was labored... and the space between breaths measured. *"Would this be the last?"*

The doctors said she was stable, but in a coma. They called it a "Gestational Diabetic Coma." This means that the pregnancy caused temporary Diabetes, and Ziven had such a low amount of sugar in her blood, that she had slipped into a coma. *"That must be why she fell and didn't attend to the stove,"* Michael thought to himself.

They said she could be in this condition for months, or could suddenly awaken at any time. They didn't offer much help... and Michael began to understand the term "practice" as it applied to physicians. It seemed that they were "practicing" on his Ziven! It was difficult for him to remain calm, but he forced himself to control his temper... for Ziven's sake.

———

Time seemed to have no meaning. Food was a nuisance. Sleep is a burden. Michael had been aware enough to call his employer so he could spend every minute of every day with Ziven in the hospital. At this point he did not care if he lost his job... he needed to be there when she woke up, no matter how long it took.

He looked over at Ziven through new eyes and he saw, for the first time, her aura. It was purely white, bright, and thick. There were beautiful rainbow colors inside that seemed to glisten and sparkle. Light rays seemed to radiate from her ever so slightly. There was a warmth and love emanating from her soul and her mind in a pure, delightful, focused and clear singular communication. She was saying, *"I love you Michael."*

The vision seemed so real. Michael woke with a start, and looked to see if Ziven was still there in the hospital bed beside him. She was... at least her body was.

Chapter IX
From Her Perspective

Ziven had been boiling some eggs and preparing the meal for Michael. Something wasn't right. She felt light-headed, so she went into the bathroom to splash some water on her face.

As she looked at her reflection in the mirror, all she could see were new wrinkles near her mouth and eyes that were not there last year. She sighed. Suddenly, honeycomb-shaped sparkles seemed to be closing in on her vision from the edge of her sight, moving inward. She grimaced, rubbed her forehead, and took a deep breath. She was light-headed and exhausted. So exhausted that she didn't feel the floor hit her as she dropped like a tree.

The only thing she could feel was the sensation of dropping below her body into some area beneath the floor... as though there were a sink hole that suddenly developed beneath her. She wasn't afraid, but instead took in the experience and let curiosity guide her impulses.

She noticed that each thought was instantly a reality. Time didn't seem to exist or pass linearly. Everything was a constant state of "now." Her body seemed to be simple, energetic and light... beautiful, warm, and invigorated. She felt infused with vitality.

She sensed her surroundings and noticed that nothing was solid. Everything was in a state of motion and fluidity. She could sense the spaces between molecules; there were no barriers. She loved the feeling of total comprehension that she had sensed in a small way before. Now, it was so much more complete and far-reaching. It was as though she had more senses and perceptions than ever before.

If she had to choose one single word to describe what she was feeling, it would be 'love.' It permeated every cell and molecule of her soul with light and warmth. It even emitted itself from "inanimate" objects. It was a delicious sensation!

Ziven heard her name. As it was spoken to her mind, it carried with it volumes of layers. It communicated exactly who she was, and how the Originator felt about, knew and understood everything about her! As He spoke her name, He communicated a deep love that had always been there and would last for the eternities. It was such a beautiful experience that she wanted to bask in that feeling forever.

The tinkling of a stream nearby drew Ziven's attention behind her. This water shimmered and spoke much more clearly than any other water she had ever seen before. Its music was more beautiful and complex than anything she had ever experienced previously in her life. It was as though fiber optics were infused into each particle, and each particle synergistically energized each particle it came in contact with. The smooth and shimmering expressions of joy were soothing, and brought a profound feeling of peace to her very soul.

It was more soothing than gazing into a fire. More relaxing than standing at the ocean shore. More comforting than wrapping up in a warm blanket on a cool evening. It was just, "more."

Ziven looked around and noticed trees and flowers surrounding her. There were so many colors! Colors she had never seen, nor even imagined before. Then, there was the music emanating from them... Each flower seemed to be singing for joy! The sound was unlike anything she had ever heard before. It was far more complete than any music she had felt from flowers before. It was calming and invigorating at the same time. She focused on the sound. They were singing songs of praise to the Creator. Their words were pure and exact. It was beautiful!

Then, Ziven noticed the trees and other foliage nearby. She could sense the living waters flowing within their veins, and could hear the orchestra of sound coming from them as they also sang songs of praise to their Creator. Every sensation available to her, and others she did not know were even possible, felt permeated with the most intense realization that love truly exists.

In the distance was a gleaming city. It seemed far away, but somehow, she knew that if she chose to go there, she could do so instantly. Somehow, she also knew that if she did that, she could not return. As she soaked in everything around her and enjoyed the feeling of utter completeness.

If only that moment could endure forever...

Ziven heard her name again... only this time it seemed as though it were coming from a tunnel somewhere far away. She felt her essence being pulled toward that tunnel; nearly against her will. It seemed almost painful to be ripped from the warmth and love she had been feeling.

The next thing she knew, she was in a strange place, on a hard surface with bright lights in her eyes and a lot of strangers with their faces circling her. She heard one of them say, "She's back!"

The next few days, Ziven was kept in the hospital for "observation." This translated to no sleep, terrible food, no privacy, and only four TV stations that came in clearly, but played game shows and talk shows. It was torture!

Michael had to return to work. Each day he would call her during his lunch break, then spend all evening with her until the morning would come, and it was time to go home to shower and get ready for work again. Ziven noticed that Michael would look her in the eyes now, whenever he was speaking to her. This was new. Part of her really liked it, and part of her didn't know what to think of it. Also, she noticed that his countenance when he looked at her was bright, and he even smiled at her sometimes.

"Could this really be true? Could he be loving me again?" She almost didn't dare to hope.

The doctors told her that the baby was unharmed by the incident. This helped calm her troubled heart a little bit, but there was this faint nagging worry that would not seem to go away completely... no matter what she did.

As soon as Ziven was released from the hospital, Michael took her to the nearest synagogue; Congregation Beth Sholom. It was unlike any synagogue she had ever seen. It had a large yellow wedge-shaped building with tall glass walls on either side. It was too modern for her taste, so she told Michael about the synagogue near Fisherman's Wharf. Now that was more like it!

It was a beautiful moment as they walked hand in hand along the streets near the Wharf, with the ocean sounds and smells, fried foods from the vendors, and the unmistakable smell of sourdough bread floating on the air. Musicians seemed to be at every corner, and as varied as the smells and sounds around them.

A steel drum musician was creatively weaving a tribal dance routine to his amazing use of mallets, rhythms, and sounds. It was mesmerizing to watch and fully engaging. Then, only a few steps away, a group of saxophones were whaling a jazzy improvisation that was stunningly beautiful and fun. The baritone saxophone had a delicious growl, the tenor saxophone was smooth and warm, and the alto saxophone made Ziven want to dance.

Just then, Michael surprised her by grabbing her around her ever-increasing waist, and began to dance with her. He had never done that before, so Ziven was stunned. It only took a moment for her to let down her defenses and simply enjoy herself.

Before long, Ziven imagined herself removed from the scene... watching herself from a distance. What a breathtaking view with the night lights of San Francisco's Fisherman's Wharf! She and her husband were dancing to jazzy saxophones. The sun was just setting over the ocean and casting brilliant colors of fire in the sky. She could see herself tossing her hair back and laughing with true abandon. *"This is definitely not a scene from our life just a month ago in Jerusalem!"* the mused.

With the glorious sunset now fading into a myriad of shades of grey, the night lights reflecting on the water, the music, and the melting pot of other sights and sounds... who could have asked for a more romantic ambiance? Well, perhaps a sunset that glistens off of the Dome of the Rock, painting all of the concrete buildings with hues of orange and yellow... but that was another life. It seemed to be a lifetime ago.

Ziven came back to herself and looked into Michael's dark brown eyes. He was smiling. She kissed him as though she would never get the chance again. She kissed him like she had never kissed him before. She kissed him, and time stood still... it was just the two of them, and she loved him. She truly loved him, and he loved her. He really did love her! Life was good... Then, came the abysmal pain...

Chapter X
Batia

Ziven buckled over, she could not stand up straight; the pain was too great. *"Yikes! Oh God of Abraham, Isaac, and Jacob! The baby is early. She can't come yet!"* Michael hailed a yellow taxi which just happened to drive by at that moment and shouted for the driver to take them to the nearest hospital.

The experienced cab driver asked which insurance they had and explained that it costs much more to go to a hospital that does not accept the proper insurance. *"What kind of world is this?"* The intense pain caught her off guard as it increased and Ziven cried, "Oh....... Please hurry!"

She didn't seem to notice the sharp turns and the quick maneuvering of the taxi as the driver darted in and out of traffic, just missing other cars by inches each time. She didn't even notice when he drove up onto the curb to avoid a collision. Michael noticed, but didn't care. At that moment, he only cared about his wife and child. Ziven was too focused on trying to get through each contraction to notice. She had been told that they hurt a lot... but she had no idea just how much. How she longed for her ima! She tried to put her worry for the baby aside, and focus on each moment. "Breathe... just breathe..." she told herself.

Michael was concerned with getting them to the hospital safely. This driver seemed fearless, and that made Michael nervous. They couldn't afford to get in an accident... not now.

Ziven was lying on a firm hospital bed with monitors and tubes connecting her to beeping machines. The pain was unbearable, but she was more concerned about their baby. It was too early... would she be alright?

"Don't push yet! The doctor's not here! He's on his way," said the nurse breathlessly as she rushed into the room.

"I can't seem to find the baby's heartbeat! It's probably just this machine. I'll bring in another one."

"No! No! No! Oh LORD, No! Please No!" Ziven shouted within herself.

"This machine is new. I must not be doing it right. I'll go get someone with more experience."

"NO!! I just want to go home! If my baby is dead, it doesn't seem fair that I still have to endure this terrible pain... for nothing!!"

"The water shows some signs of distress. This isn't a good sign."

"Ouch! It hurts!! I just want to go home and cry! Can't I just leave this horrible pain on the table and go home?! What did I do wrong? Did I eat something that caused this? Is JEHOVAH punishing me for some past sin?"

"Don't push yet! The doctor is here and he's washing his hands."

The nurse told the doctor, "I'm picking up the mother's heartbeat on the fetal monitor. This is strange."

"Ouch!! I don't want to go through all of this if I cannot go home with my baby! I WANT TO GO HOME TO CRY! I WANT TO BE ALONE!!!"

The doctor said, "The image doesn't look good. The baby's heart is not beating."

Michael looked into Ziven's golden eyes that were swollen and red from crying. They had so much fear and a desperate look to them. He felt a wave of intense compassion... and helplessness. He pushed aside his own sorrow and anguish to help her get through this. He had been holding her hand, but then began to stroke her long brown hair. This seemed to calm her breathing a little bit, so he continued.

"Ziven, I love you. We will get through this," he said tenderly. She found some comfort in his gaze. It was almost healing. Almost.

The soberness in the room was as thick as Kugel pudding, but not as sweet. Everyone who looked at Ziven and Michael, could not keep eye contact... but would look away immediately. That would make her feel even lonelier, except that she had Michael... she had Michael...

The recovery room they put her in was near all of the other new mothers in the hospital. She could hear them cooing and loving their new babies. It was torture.

The nurse brought in their little girl. They had decided to name her "Batia" which means "Daughter of God." Indeed she was, and now they were required to give her back to Him, by JEHOVAH's will.

She was wrapped up tightly in a scratchy white blanket with a blue stripe and a pink stripe. She had lots of dark black hair like her father, and high cheek bones like her mother. Curiously, she also had a square jaw like her grandfather and perfect lips like her grandmother. Her hands and feet were perfect, Ziven carefully inspected her beloved baby.

Ziven found this to be curious and questioned whether she was imagining it, or if it were simply a coincidence. Certainly, she was a good mix. Her skin was bluish purple... but she looked so peaceful... as if she were sleeping.

Michael could not bring himself to touch the dead body of his little daughter. It was tradition in Jerusalem that the dead are taken care of by the "holy society" (chevra kaddisha). One would go the long way around a burial area to avoid stepping near a cemetery because even being in the presence of the dead would make one "spiritually unclean," and require a ritualistic cleansing of the hands before entering any home.

It didn't take very long before Michael just wanted to go home to cry himself. The compassionate nurses moved Ziven to a regular recovery room so she wouldn't have to hear the other mothers with their newborn infants. Michael knew Ziven would be alright. He needed to go home. He needed time to think. Time to let down his guard and cry. Time to pray.

That night the grey skies produced a tremendous thunderstorm. Normally, Ziven adored thunderstorms. She loved to stand outside and let the wind blow through her hair, watch the patterns of light in the sky, and feel the ions in the air just before a thunder strike. But, today was different. This day made all future days seem bleak.

She stood at the window and watched the cars far below... driving through the storm... on their merry way... as though everything was fine. But it was NOT fine! How could they go on with their lives as though nothing happened? Something DID happen! Her life had just crumbled around her, and they were down there driving by as though everything was fine! She felt angry and turned away from the window to wallow in despair.

Ziven sobbed unabashedly into her pillow until there were no more tears. Exhausted, she lay there looking at the ceiling.

Suddenly, a pure thought pierced through the fog of her mind into her heart, *"Dear daughter, everything will be alright."* She felt a warm tingling sensation start at her head and drench her entire body. She took a deep breath and felt strangely peaceful and calm. She didn't know how, but she trusted that feeling that everything really would be alright... eventually everything would truly be alright!

Late that night, Ziven was awakened by the nurses who were visiting just outside of her door. She sighed and rolled over to try to go back to sleep. She sensed someone sitting in the chair next to her bed... She looked, but saw no one. Could she be imagining it? She had the same feeling again... so, ever curious, she let herself explore that possibility.

She closed her eyes and could see in her mind an adult woman near her side. She had long dark brown wavy hair. Her complexion was clear and olive. Her eyes were golden and full of love. In one instant the following was communicated to Ziven by this shadowy visitor:

"I'm your daughter. I love you! Everything will be alright. I honor you as my mother. You will have another child who will live to give you grandchildren. This posterity will rise up and call you blessed."

Then, it was over. Ziven instantly understood her daughter's personality. She was fun-loving and bubbly, but also serious. She was extremely intelligent, artistic, and loved to laugh. She had a wisdom that was deeply profound. Her soul seemed ancient but childlike.

Ziven took a deep breath and let it cleanse her mind. *"Wow!"* she thought. At that instant, her body was flooded with that same warm tingly sensation that seemed to confirm the validity of what had just happened. She smiled and drifted off to sleep; a wonderfully deep and rejuvenating sleep. A sleep that was more peaceful and lovely than she had experienced for a very long time. A very—long—time.

The next few days were spent making arrangements for the burial of their little one at the cemetery near the North Beach Chabad Synagogue on Lombard Street near Fisherman's Wharf.

They wrapped sweet Batia in a tallit according to Jewish burial custom. Ziven threw in a handful of soil from the Holy Land into the grave, also according to custom.

Michael could not bring himself to come, so Ziven had to take care of everything by herself. On the tombstone, in Hebrew, were the words, "Our Beloved Firstborn – Returned to God".

Chapter XI
Atohi

The following months were a blur. Ziven and Michael both went through each day emotionless. At the end of the day, they each sat in the same room like mannequins and only spoke to each other as necessary. No sadness. No joy. Nothing. They rarely ate, and when they did, they both just picked at it and then went into the living room to turn on the TV. It didn't dull the pain as they had hoped, but it was something that could make it less uncomfortable for them to just sit there not looking at or talking to each other... until it was time to go silently to bed and try to escape.

Every day, Ziven would take the streetcar to Lombard Street and sit on a bench near Batia's grave side. She would sit numbly day after day... not moving... not speaking... not feeling... until it was time to return to prepare dinner for Michael before he returned home from work.

She refused to ceremoniously wash her hands before entering her home because she didn't feel unclean. She knew she couldn't tell Michael, though, because he would never understand. He didn't carry their child within him for 7 months. He hadn't had the sweet experience she had with the spirit of their daughter. He was too "Orthodox."

One day, Ziven decided to walk along Fisherman's Wharf and heard a new sound... It was a haunting sound... It was a type of music she had never heard before; some sort of flute.

She felt drawn toward that sound and followed it until she came to a pier that was away from the hustle and bustle of the main area of the Wharf. Seagulls were calling and the ocean waves were lapping against the pier. An old man stood alone, playing a wooden flute toward Alcatraz Island.

The notes he played trailed off at the end of each phrase which gave the melody a mournful feel to it, ancient and sweet. The melodies were strange and different from anything she had ever heard before.

Ziven just stood there listening to the music, for it awakened within her something that had been asleep deep within her. So deep that it seemed like the Bay fog was not only burning off as the sun came up, but a fog was lifting from her mind and soul.

"That was just beautiful! How does it work? It looks different from other wooden flutes I've seen in my country," Ziven braved.

The old Native American looked into her soul through her eyes, smiled and motioned for her to sit near him on a nearby log.

He said, "You not from here," with a twinkle in his eye and a slight smile in one corner of his mouth.

Ziven thought her "American" accent was under control.

Disappointed that she didn't blend in, she answered, "I am from Israel. Jerusalem actually."

The old man looked into her eyes and smiled. "No," he said. You Native American, but did not grow up here."

"How did he know???" Ziven suddenly felt very exposed and uncomfortable.

The old man said, "Please forgive, but I see Cherokee in your face. My mother Cherokee. My father Ohlone. They became part of 'Indians of All Tribes' and met at Alcatraz." This put her at ease, and she suddenly felt safe.

"My name is Ziven.... but the name I was given as a child is 'Gwenelda.'"

The old man's deep wrinkles increased as he smiled and asked, "What you want I call you?"

"Gwenelda, please. And what may I call you?" she asked. "I 'Atohi' because I speak with the trees."

Ziven felt a connection with this old man, as though they had known each other for centuries. She looked at his deeply creviced wrinkles, and the streaks of grey at his temples in his long braided hair. His face wore the evidence of many years of both smiling and frowning. His eyes were green with golden flecks that gave him the look of piercing into the soul. His body was thin and frail looking, but his arms appeared to be lean and strong.

She imagined that he was ruggedly handsome when he was young. She wondered how old he really was. There was no way to tell unless she asked him... and she didn't plan to do that.

Atohi looked into Ziven's eyes, sizing her up, and said, "You speak with the trees too." Ziven laughed in surprise. "It's more like they speak with me." The old man nodded in approval and chuckled to himself. Then, Ziven spilled her story.

She told him about where she grew up. She told him about how she found out her real name. She told him about talking with the trees. She told him about the bombing that killed her parents. She told him about her hopes of a new life here with Michael. And she told him about the death of her daughter Batia.

She wondered why it was that she felt so connected with this stranger; so comfortable that she would share such personal things with him.

Atohi listened intently looking into her soul and nodded occasionally with a slight grunt of understanding. By now, the sky was dark. Ziven suddenly realized that Michael would be home by now, and wondered where she was. She quickly began gathering her things when the old man said, "Come again tomorrow and I show you something beautiful."

Ziven thanked the old fossil and rushed off to catch a trolley car to the BART system. She tried to call Michael, but got his voicemail. She didn't leave a message; what would she say? (I spent all evening pouring out my life's story to a stranger on the pier?) He would think she was crazy... maybe she was... but for the first time in months she felt alive again.

The next morning, she got ready early and made her way to Fisherman's Wharf. She didn't stop to visit Batia's grave, she just went directly to the Wharf. She felt driven to find Atohi.

He was in the same spot waiting for her and smiled as she excitedly approached. "I want share something beautiful with you." Then he stood up and without saying a word began to walk down the sidewalk. Confused, Ziven followed him.

Eventually, they came to a bus stop and waited for 5 minutes. The old man stood there looking straight ahead without speaking. Ziven's curiosity began to take control and she watched the ancient one and wondered what "beautiful" thing he wanted to show her.

They took a bus to nearby Muir Woods. Ziven gasped as she stepped out of the bus. The beautiful, Giant Redwood Sequoia trees were breathtaking!

The haunting whistle of the Varied Thrush, with its bright yellow and black feathers was carried on a gentle breeze. The chirps and music of chickadees and various sparrows added a delicious excitement to the air; while the lovely complexity of the Winter Wren song added to the exuberant joy known only to birds of the redwoods.

Atohi watched Ziven carefully. She beamed at him in thanks and then began walking down the gravel path. She couldn't help but look up, up, up.

The deep brownish-red bark of the trees drew the gaze upward 350 feet to where the blue sky was finally able to reach the flat pine needles. There was a feeling of ancient calm there, and the ground seemed sacred.

Ziven breathed in deep the refreshing smell of moist earth, wood, and understory. She sensed new wisdom that comes from being in the presence of trees that are thousands of years old. She imagined the things that they must have seen: Native Peoples, Spanish explorers, Pioneers, The Gold Rush, Pony Express, Civil War, Transcontinental Railroad, earthquakes, Alcatraz Island events, Golden Gate Bridge, horse-and-buggy to cars and tourists... They would have had to witness everything she had read about America in that area.

She stopped near a 3,000 year old tree, tentatively reached out her hand and gently touched its 20-inch thick bark. The etchings of the bark were so deep! The circumference of the trunk was nearly 100 feet! As Ziven shared with the behemoth her profound respect and gratitude, she suddenly felt the flow of information change direction!

The "Guardian" as he called himself shared an everlasting love for all creation. He reveled in the songs and lives of the forest birds and animals. He enjoyed watching people of all ages and times walking among his family in these sacred woods. The life-giving water shimmered deep within the Guardian's veins, each molecule making its way to the precious cones with seeds of future generations. These cones would not be released for many years, but in the meantime, every drop of water in the foggy mists, every drop of shimmering water deep within the soil or flowing in streams nearby, and every drop of moisture that fell from the sky was captured and absorbed – cherished and adored by these great ones.

Ziven told the trees that she was honored to be in their presence. They smiled. She could hear them all singing praises to the Creator. They were singing music full of joy and rejoicing. Their deep tones and melodies were smooth and flowing. The chords were constant with occasional modifications from some of the trees that changed the entire feel of the harmonies. The feeling of reverberating sound seemed to fill the air with vibrations that she imagined could be felt across the ocean to her homeland of Israel and around the entire earth. It was the most beautiful sound Ziven had ever heard! It filled her soul with a peaceful happiness that was energized and full of warm light.

Everywhere she turned, she could hear the music; the beautiful music that was almost not of this world. Haunting chord structures and complex melodies. All saying the same thing, *"Praise God!"*

Each step Ziven took on the understory seemed to light up in a pulse of electrically connected oneness. She felt linked in a golden chain of time that joined her to their history as a welcome guest. No, it was more like she was a long-lost family member, welcomed home.

She turned to Atohi and breathlessly said, "Thank you for bringing me here!" tears spilling from her eyes. Atohi understood. He could hear the music as well. He smiled so broadly, exposing his darkened teeth with some missing. Ziven almost expected his face to crack by virtue of the intensified wrinkles that developed on his face.

They spent the next few hours walking along the prescribed paths, delighting in the squirrels and birds, the gentle salty breeze, and the songs of the trees... Atohi also showed Ziven many of the native plant life that saved his people from starvation, many of the naturally growing herbs and their medicinal effects. She found it fascinating, but her heart was full of so much love that all she could think of was getting home to Michael. She needed to tell him how much she loved him. Her heart ached to be with him at this moment.

On his way home from work that day, Michael let his mind ponder over how things had been at home the past few months since Batia was born... well, not exactly born because she never took a breath... but the distance between Ziven and him seemed to grow. They expressed no feelings toward each other... They simply existed in the same home, like two strangers. It was causing a deepening ache within him.

Subconsciously, he felt like a failure. How could he be a good provider, a good husband, a protector, if he couldn't be there for his wife in her time of need? He began to try to see things from her perspective; this was a new concept for him.

A door of understanding suddenly opened, like a floodgate. Ziven just needed to feel loved. She needed to feel connected to him. She must feel so very lonely. She must ache for compassion and tenderness from her only family – him. He was all she had. She was all he had. They only had each other.

Michael spent the rest of the time thinking about ways he could show Ziven that he loved her. He made a mental list of all the things he could think of, like: helping with the dishes, picking up his dirty socks, clearing his place at the table, thanking her for the meal, telling her she looks pretty, holding her spontaneously and telling her that he loves her, looking into her eyes and then kissing her 'just because,' stroking her arm or back whenever near her, brushing her hair, massaging her back, opening doors for her and letting her go through first, holding out her chair for her, asking her if there is anything that needs fixing around the house and then repairing it, taking her out on a date weekly, kissing her hello and goodbye whenever leaving or returning to their house, reading the Torah together, going for walks (hand in hand) in the evenings, asking her about her day, finding one way to serve her each day, etc.

It is customary in Jerusalem for the woman to be supportive of the man of the house. It is not generally thought that the man should work hard to make the woman happy... but then again, Ziven was no ordinary woman... and this (after all) was America.

The list was long, but it helped him to have a mental list to draw from. He felt gratified that he could think of so many possibilities. He was feeling like he could be a good husband and make his beautiful bride feel happy and loved again. Perhaps he could make her smile, or even laugh again. This anticipation made him quicken his step as he made his way home. He was excited to see Ziven. It has been a long time. *"Perhaps she will be glad to see me too,"* he thought.

Chapter XII
Trail of Tears

Every day, while Michael was at work, Ziven would go into town to visit Atohi. *"What is it about this old man that I am so drawn to him?"*

They talked about the history of the Cherokee People. Ziven's heart was drawn out in sorrow for the Trail of Tears they had to endure.

Atohi had a special gift when it came to storytelling. He made you feel as though you were actually there. "Long ago, in the 1830's" he began, "when corn stalks reached 9 feet into sky, and white soldiers forced 'Real People' to leave homes. They left log homes and clapboard homes to go to new place where nothing waited for them. They would have to start over again."

"The 'Real People' were very sad as they walking... walking and women crying... children crying for food... many tears. Everyone crying. Big tears. Corn bent over and touched ground. Corn was crying with 'Real People' every day...corn crying... people crying."

"New plants that grew from the tears could not reach sky. The corn seeds are sad with grief of 'Real People' and color is now color of sorrow. Even shape of corn seeds are shape of tears."

Atohi smiled as he brought forth a leather bag with a drawstring tie and handed it to Ziven. He motioned for her to take the heartfelt gift. Humbled, Ziven loosened the leather drawstring to open the bag and find a beautiful bead necklace. It had gold beads, precious stone beads, and corn seed beads. The corn seeds were tear shaped and smoky grey in color.

"This corn bead necklace for you to remember your people," he said. "Thank you, Atohi!" Ziven rushed into the old man's arms and hugged him. The tears began to flow as she could feel the corn beads transfer the essence of the story she had just heard into her subconscious. "Thank you!" she whispered as she tried to control the tears from freely flowing.

Afterwards, Ziven caught control of her emotions... she put the necklace on over her head and asked Atohi, "Will you please tell me more about what you know about the 'Trail of Tears'? What was it really like for our people?"

The moment Ziven said "our people" she felt a warm chill start at her head and drench her body to her toes. The realization that she was Cherokee and learning more about her heritage drew her heart like a swift river nearing a waterfall. She wanted, she needed to learn more... and this dear old man with the twinkle in his eye was her link to her past and to her future.

In her studies, Ziven learned that there were 10 million Native Americans on the northern American continent when the first non-Natives arrived. Over the course of the next 300 years, 90% of all Native American original population was either wiped out by disease, famine, or warfare with the white man. That's nine million dead!

She had also read as much as she could find on the Trail of Tears. There was nothing available in Jerusalem libraries, but the Internet provided her with basic facts. (She had learned that the Internet in the United States was actually un-restricted, unfiltered, and had enjoyed its use at the library as well as the vast choices of reference books available there.)

Ziven had learned that the Trail of Tears covered more than 2,200 miles of land and water and involved nine states. She had heard that the son of the main chief of the Cherokees was actually a law student at Princeton when President Andrew Jackson called for the removal of the Civilized Tribes to Oklahoma. There was a lot of evidence that it was motivated by the natural resources found in their current lands and the greed and corruption of the leaders of that time.

Atohi began, "My mother carried me, wrapped to her breast, a new baby on the Trail of Tears. She say I cry much because she not make enough milk."

"Many old womens, and sick peoples carry heavy packs on their backs. They walk on frozen ground with rags on their bleeding feet. The Real Peoples were 15,000. The white man divided us into 13 groups to leave every three days on same path. Before we left, they walked through our houses to see what they wanted to keep and what we could take. Mother had china plates we traded for. She cried to leave them. White men were in our house, taking her things as we left. White man kill cattle and hogs. Some burn houses down if Peoples not leave."

"Other Peoples had to leave too: Chickasaws, Choctaws, Creeks, and Seminoles. About 100,000 of us all together. Many tears. Much sorrow. Many died every day. We treated like animals. Some Peoples in chains. Treaties were broken. Many angry. Want to fight. Many want peace. Much confusion."

"Many days pass and peoples die very much. Five people each day left behind to go to the Great Spirit home. Very thirsty. Very hungry. Soldiers not kind. Not given time to take books or toys."

"Some of the Real Peoples went other way and trapped between frozen rivers. Womens cry and make sad wails. Children cry and many mens cry, but they say nothing and just put heads down and keep on going towards West. Many days pass and peoples die very much. Drink dirty water and die every day. Over 4,000 die."

"White soldier wagons gave little bit of food: cornbread, green corn, and sometimes some buffalo, but sometimes three days no water. No trails, so mens and womens cut trees with axes for soldier's wagons."

"Old womens and mens too weak to keep up, were left behind to die alone. Children cried for their mothers and fathers and grandparents, left behind to die. Some womens have new babies that died soon after, and some womens died too."

"When Real Peoples die, no time to honor them with ceremony. Just put dead bodies in a tree or covered with bushes. Some not covered, just left for the animals to make meat of."

"Some mens carried reeds with eagle feathers from the medicine men to encourage the Real Peoples not to be so sorrowful, and not to think of the homes they left behind."

"Some older womens sang songs that meant, 'We are going to our new homes and land. There is One Who is above and ever watches over us. He will take care of us.' Then they have little bit of hope."

Ziven was overcome with emotion and was sobbing uncontrollably now. She looked around her at the people bustling about. It was as though they suddenly appeared and had been nowhere near while Atohi shared the history of their people.

She said, "Have you ever noticed how everyone is always in such a hurry?"

"What could be so important?" she rhetorically asked under her breath. Atohi gave her a moment to recover and then said, "Come back tomorrow, my child. I share something very special with you." Then, the old man smiled, stood up and walked away without looking back. Ziven thought this was a bit odd, but she had gotten used to the old man's peculiarities

Chapter XIII
The Bloodwood Flute

That evening, when Michael got home from work, he walked up the entry to their home and was distracted by the beautiful roses growing along the path. He stopped to pick the largest one, smelled it and smiled.

Ziven would be waiting for him inside. He would take her into his arms and swing her around, tell her he loved her desperately, and then kiss her. Well, that was the plan.

As he entered the front door, he smelled something sweet like honey, butter, and pecans.... Could it be his favorite dessert? Could it be baklava?! Ziven came out of the kitchen with her hair pulled back, a cooking apron, and flour splotches on her face. Michael's jaw dropped. She was beautiful as she brought a plate of fresh, warm, sticky, baklava to the dining room table.

Michael was breathless too... but it was at seeing Ziven looking so beautiful and happy to see him. "You are a vision!" he managed to say. Ziven blushed.

Michael offered her the rose from the front yard, then pulled her into his arms and began dancing American-style dancing. She teasingly put the rose between her teeth, so he started dancing a Tango.

Ziven threw her head back and laughing said, "Where did you learn to dance like this?" Michael swung her around and then held her in a long low lunge and said in his best American accent, "I paid attention to all of those 'chick flicks' you thought I was sleeping through."

She smiled and he began kissing her. Then, they fell to the floor laughing... the first time that laughter had been heard in their new American home... and the first time laughter had been heard between the two of them in a very long time. He exclaimed, "Oof!" as they fell, to which Ziven quipped, "I heard that!" Then, the giggling began.

The next morning when Ziven woke up, she laid in bed and stretched, smiling. The morning sun was shining in through her bedroom window, and she didn't even notice the dust dancing in the air. She took a deep breath and rubbed her eyes. She felt complete and happy.

Suddenly she remembered that Atohi said he wanted to share something special with her. She sprang out of bed, threw some comfortable clothes on, and was out the door within 5 minutes.

He was waiting for her at the Wharf, in his usual spot, playing his flute. The San Francisco Bay fog was still clinging to the water and gave a misty backdrop to the old man and his music. It was quite stunning, and the haunting melody captivated Ziven and stopped her in her tracks until he was finished. The music seemed to speak to her soul in an amazingly profound way. Atohi smiled and motioned for Ziven to sit on the nearby log with him.

He loosened the leather strap that was holding the "bird" to the flute and revealed two rectangular holes connected with a very thin shaft or flue at the head of the flute. He handed the wooden flute to Ziven.

The Ebony wood was black, heavy and smooth. It was so smooth it could almost be described as "soft." She felt the hole at the end of the flute and could not feel a seam inside. She wondered if the hole was drilled directly in the center, or if there were two halves put together perfectly.

The mouthpiece was shaped like a large cigar, smooth and rounded. The finger holes were different sizes and not exactly in a straight line. The barrel was as shiny as polished metal. The designs were simple stripes with inlaid crushed precious stones, like black obsidian lined with yellow, bluish-green turquoise, and red coral.

The piece of wood that had been held tight to the flute (the bird) was actually not a bird shape at all. It looked more like a brown bear. Some polished turquoise, coral, and other gems were inlaid into the side of the bear. It had been carved into a basic shape, but still had some details and texture that made it beautiful. It was a lighter color than the deep black of the Ebony wood.

There were special holes near the bear's feet that thin leather straps were threaded through. They held the shape of the bear securely over one of the holes and on top of the flue. Ziven looked up at Atohi in wonder. She had heard him play before, but had never really seen the flute up close. He had always slipped it into his bag as she was walking up to him, so she was never really close enough to take a real look at it.

Certainly, she had not imagined the weight of the wood which seemed out of proportion with the size of the wood. The smooth Ebony shined in Ziven's hands as she tilted it and turned it to see the patterns of the dark grain. It was truly a thing of beauty.

Then, Ziven was surprised as she began to sense something from the flute itself. This was not something she expected. *"I am very old, but I used to be filled with life and light. The old man made me and gave me new life. I can sing songs of praise to the Creator because of him, and I am so grateful."*

Ziven looked at Atohi, and he just smiled that "knowing smile" of his. He pointed with his lips for her to tighten the straps and try to play his beloved flute. She felt the flute give its approval as well. No words were needed. Ziven simply understood.

She tightened the leather straps and looked to Atohi to see if she had placed the bird correctly over the correct chamber of the flute.

He nodded and pointed with his lips again. She then put the flute to her mouth and blew gently.

A lovely resonance replaced the shrill squeak she expected. Ziven had never been very musical and had no confidence that she could create such a beautiful sound... but she did. It was truly lovely.

Atohi smiled even more broadly and said to Ziven, "I show you how to make flute for you. Then I show how to play like Cherokee Princess." He said that last part with a wink, for there is no such thing as a "Cherokee Princess," per se. The white man assumed that the daughter of a Cherokee chief should be called a princess... but the truth is; every Cherokee father called his daughter "princess" because he thought she was the most beautiful of all, and he loved her the best.

Ziven remembered that she had shared with him the day she found out she was Cherokee, and her mother had called her a "Cherokee Princess." She smiled excitedly and rushed to keep up with the old man who had already begun walking down the sidewalk.

His walk was brisker than she remembered. That was fine with her, for she was excited to make a flute of her own. It was beyond anything she had ever dreamed of; an experience she would not have imagined could be hers. *My own Native American flute!*

The floor of the wood shop was covered with dust and shavings of all colors. The sun shining in through the window revealed dust particles dancing in the air. The smell was warm and earthy. Ziven actually liked it. There were tools hanging on hooks all over the wall. They were neatly organized by shape and style. In the corner was a stack of pieces of wood. Some of it was cut into 6 X 2 X 8 lengths, while there were all sorts of other sizes of bits and pieces of wood from other projects. They were stacked neatly by size and color.

This was a part of Atohi that Ziven would never have guessed. Atohi said, "Choose wood. We make flute for Ziven."

"Wow!" she exclaimed under her breath, and she began to look through the stack of wood. A warm comfortable feeling overcame Ziven as she began to glimpse communications from the wood. One piece in particular seemed to call out to her more than the others. It was a deep reddish-brown color.

As she held it in the sunlight, she could see shimmering veins of bright gold. It took her breath away. The piece of wood was warped and twisted. The weight of it felt heavy like the ebony, and the touch of it was cold and hard.

Ziven smiled at Atohi and questioned with her eyes if she could use this one. The old man hefted the piece of wood and eyed the length of it. "This one not straight... but..." he added "extra work, make beautiful flute. You see."

Ziven said, "It is twisted and warped, but it is so beautiful! Are you sure it will work?" Atohi snorted as he nodded to give emphasis that yes, of course he could make it work. "It's perfect," she replied.

"They said I am 'twisted and warped'... is that bad? I think it is because I made room for the little evergreen tree. Now it is difficult to remain straight. Will I ever be useful again? When the woman picked me up and said I was 'beautiful!' She said she loved the way my veins shine when the sunlight illuminates them. She said I was 'perfect.' The old man told her that I was 'twisted and warped.' Then he said that with a lot of work, they could make a nice flute out of me. I did not understand exactly what a 'flute' was, but it sounded like something good."

"What kind of wood is this, and where does it grow?" she asked the old man. "Bloodwood." he answered. "Grows in South America. Bleeds when it is cut."

Atohi selected a board of Curly Maple. It had lovely cream-colored patterns in its grain that swirled around like a whirlpool of water. Atohi's plan was to show Ziven how to make her flute by watching him make one of his own.

The old man used a ruler to measure and draw a straight line on the wood. He used a vice to hold the board still, and a hand saw to cut two identical lengths. Then, he did the same to Ziven's wood.

"First, we need make straight." He motioned to her pieces of wood. A large block of marble had a strip of sandpaper attached to it. Atohi showed Ziven how to scrape the wood in long, slow motions, the length of the sandpaper. She was to do this to both sides and measure the thickness on each end until they were equal.

Before long, Ziven's arms were growing tired, but she didn't mind. *"This flute is going to be beautiful! Wait until Michael sees this!"* she thought.

Atohi used a pencil to make more measured marks on all of the pieces. Then, he pulled down two rounded chisels from the wall, handed one to Ziven and motioned for her to do what he was doing.

He was chiseling two troughs or channels. One was short, and the other was long and went through to the end of the wood. Next Atohi pencil sketched two rectangular marks and some lines between them. He explained that he had to do this part himself because it had to be perfect, or the flute would not work.

Then he handed a small flat chisel to Ziven and showed her how to make a 45° angle in the two rectangular holes. You couldn't see this feature from the top of the flute once it was finished, but it seemed critical.

The next few hours flew by like the wind. Atohi and Ziven quietly worked on the wood; removing all the parts that were not "flute." Touching the wood, carving, sanding, and more sanding with sandpaper that was finer and finer... was a very grounding experience for Ziven. She would never have thought that such a connection could be made with a piece of wood.

"I desperately tried to tell the woman my story. I told her about how I used to be part of a living tree, but was cut off. I tried to sing a song of praise for the Creator, but could not. I was just about to give up when I could feel her

communicating with me! She was the first human I have ever met who could share her thoughts with me. It was exhilarating! She said that she had been cut off as well... cut off from the presence of the Creator. She asked me to trust her. She said that she would help me to sing again. Oh, how I wanted to sing again! I agreed, and she thanked me. The next thing I knew, the old man was showing her how to use strange tools to cut and carve me. She kept asking me to trust her. She made me straight again by shaving off some of my red wood. She cut out a deep groove, and then another, and another. She used many types of sand paper to make those grooves very smooth. She would hum to the old man while sanding me. She has a beautiful voice! Oh how I wish I could join her and sing praises again! She told me to be patient, and to trust her. She said she loves me. She said I am beautiful! I feel happy!"

Once the grooves were carved and smoothed, Atohi smiled and said with childlike excitement, "Now for powerful love glue!" and he winked. Ziven looked at the bottle of "Gorilla Glue" and wondered when the old man had discovered this way to make his flute-building more effective. She also wondered about his story behind calling it "powerful love glue."

They carefully placed a small strip of glue along all edges, smoothed it with their fingers, pressed the two pieces of wood together with small clamps, wiped the excess glue that squeezed out, and then tied the planks together so they could not move. Then, they wrapped a rag around a dowel and wiped the excess glue from the inside of the long chamber. *"So that's how it became so smooth and seamless inside,"* Ziven mused.

It would be a week before the next step of making the flute could be attempted. Since it was time to go home anyway, Ziven collected her purse to leave. Michael would be home soon and would be hungry.

On the way home, Ziven rehearsed in her mind the connection she had felt with the Bloodwood. It seemed to awaken within her a more profound yearning to investigate and become part of the heritage of her Cherokee bloodline.

That evening, when Michael walked in the door, he looked particularly tired. Ziven asked, "How was your day?"

She loved it that she was actually interested in his answer. This was new. She liked their new relationship. He was trying. He was aware of her. He looked her in the eyes when he spoke to her and had stopped talking down to her. He seemed to have a tenderness in his expression when he looked at her. She was no longer invisible.

Michael spoke of politics at work. That is to say, there is a hierarchy and un-written laws that are not always evident to the new guy. His English was improving quite a bit, but the American way of business was a little more difficult for him to grasp than he had anticipated.

No one had explained the social rules to him; he had to figure it all out the hard way... and it was difficult. Ziven stepped behind the sofa he was sitting on and began rubbing Michael's shoulders to help him relax. "Hmmmmm. That feels good." he said; his eyes closed.

Ziven said, "Michael, I want you to know that I appreciate that you go to work every day to pay the bills. I know it is not easy. Thank you." Michael startled Ziven as he spun around to greet her eyes, and said, "I want you to know that I appreciate YOU." Ziven thought to herself, *"Whatever could I be doing that he appreciates?"* and gave him a puzzled look.

He began again, "You have made this house a warm inviting HOME. When I come home from work, I am glad to come home because you are here. I love you with all of my heart." Then, he pulled her to him and made her fall onto the sofa. Her brown hair that had begun to collect streaks of golden highlights flew in all directions as she landed breathless and laughing. Her eyes were bright and smiling at him with the light of love.

This was the Ziven he fell in love with. She thought he was going to kiss her, but he started a tickling war instead until they were both laughing so hard they could not stop. Dinner was cold that night, but Ziven didn't care. She and Michael were happy.

The next week when Ziven met Atohi at the usual place, he looked old. It's not that he didn't look old before... but she never saw his wrinkles as more than evidence of a life well-lived. Today he looked... what was the word... "frail."

He moved slowly as they walked to the wood shop where the flutes-to-be had been drying into one solid piece of wood. Ziven noticed that Atohi did not step "heel-toe" like everyone else. His steps were "toe-heel."

Curious, she asked him about it. "Why do you step toe first?" Atohi chuckled and said, "I not know. My grandfather taught me walk this way. I think to sneak up on deer when hunting." That made sense.

Ziven tried walking toe first and noticed a tremendous difference in the sound her shoes were making. There is much I can learn from this old man." she thought to herself. "I'm so glad I met him!"

"Grandfather," she said to him... "You are moving slowly today. Are you feeling well enough to work on the flutes today?"

"I am fine, my child. The flutes do not want wait any longer."

He was right about that... and neither could Ziven wait. She was excited to connect with her roots by working with this branch of red wood. They worked quietly at removing the sharp edges with a hand plainer. Ziven found herself humming a strange new tune. She seemed to be humming in tandem with the flute.

"I'm imagining this," she said to herself as she continued to hum and work at smoothing the edges. Atohi sat Ziven at what looked like a lathe, only it was operated with a belt and pedal much like a spinning wheel. She was to pump her foot on the pedal to make it spin. The flute was attached to the device horizontally and would spin faster as she pumped the pedal quicker.

Ziven was given a sharp blade and was amazed at how little bits of the edges of the wood would come flying off by simply holding the blade steady and spinning the flute in place. She seemed to sense that the flute was confused and worried about what was happening to it... so she began to comfort the flute.

It was a beautiful bonding that was taking place. A very strong bond was building between them. Perhaps this is what the old man meant by the "powerful love glue." A profound love was growing between Ziven and the Bloodwood flute as they communicated while she was shaping and preparing it to be beautifully smooth.

"I didn't see the woman for many days. When she returned, she put me on a machine that made me spin around. While I was spinning, I felt a sharp tool shave small pieces of my wood away. I felt dizzy, confused, and afraid. The woman just kept saying, 'You will sing again... just trust me a little while longer. Trust me...' Then I said, 'I trust you. Thank you for helping me. Thank you for loving me. I will do my best to show my love for you too.'"

Ziven worked for many hours, humming and sanding, sanding and humming, until the flute began to take shape. The old man helped her drill holes and tune them.

Then, he had her choose a small piece of wood from a different pile. He said, "It needs be softer wood to soak up breath water." She understood. She chose a lovely piece of wood that was honey colored and had pretty brown stripes.

"Is this ok?" she asked. Atohi nodded. "What kind of wood is this?" "It Alligator Juniper," he responded. Then, he chose a small piece of wood for his own flute and they began carving... carving.

They used the marble slab to sand the bottom until it was perfectly flat. "If not flat, flute no play," he explained. Then was the magical moment... Ziven put her lips to the Bloodwood flute and gently blew.

The last thing to do was to seal everything with oil. Atohi said, "Tomorrow, we cover with oil and decorate to make more pretty."

It was getting late, and Ziven didn't know if she could wait another day to show Michael. She would play it for him, and he would be so pleased.

Chapter XIV
The Clean Wood Shop

The next few days, Ziven could not meet Atohi. She had several errands to run for Michael that could not wait. A deposit at the bank, shopping for groceries since there was no food in their home, shopping for some specific clothes he needed for work, dropping off a package in the mail, and other tasks that needed to be done during the day.

Finally, she was able to go to the Wharf to meet Atohi. She hoped he would be there. She hoped he wouldn't be disappointed that she took so many days to meet him to finish her flute.

Excited, she made her way on the Wharf to the familiar place where she first met the old man... but he wasn't there. She looked everywhere, but he was nowhere to be found!

Ziven asked local vendors and musicians if they had seen him. No one had seen him for several days. Worry began to set in as she made her way to the wood shop where they had been making the flutes.

The door was partially opened, (not a good sign) so she walked in calling for Atohi. The place was very clean. Too clean. Not one tool was out of place. There was no dust floating in the air and the floor was perfectly clean. Something was terribly wrong!

The old man's apartment was above the wood shop somewhere... so Ziven began looking for it. What she found was a landlord instead. He was a very large burly man with bronzed skin, dark curly hair, and a T-shirt that was far too small for his enormous frame, bulging arms and large stomach.

Tokoni was obviously Tongan and appeared to be about 30 years old. His large lips and short nose were set squarely in the center of his large round face. He was eating an apple and talking easily while a large bite of food was splashing around in his wide open mouth, making a smacking sound and spitting out juice as he spoke.

Ziven asked if he knew what had happened to Atohi. Tokoni told her that the old man had been found dead in his bed three nights before. He had apparently died of old age in his sleep. He had not appeared to have experienced any pain. He had no family that they knew of, so they had cremated his body, and were going to spread his ashes in the ocean.

Ziven sat down quickly, her head was spinning and she felt ill. "Dead? He's dead?" is all she could say. "Oh Great Father... No!" Tokoni asked, "Were you close to him?" Her head down and her eyes a tearful glaze she whispered, barely audibly, "Yes. We were very close."

"Then, perhaps you would like to spread his ashes." the tall Tongan offered. Ziven nodded. She could not speak. She found herself walking numbly with the almost finished wooden flute in one hand, and a tin can full of ashes in the other. She eventually found herself at the very spot on the wharf where she first met Atohi.

She wasn't sure how she got there. She didn't remember anything about walking that way, or taking a bus, or anything else. Suddenly, she realized where she was. This was where she always found him... but he was no longer there.

Ziven sat down and stared at the horizon. The familiar sights and sounds of the busy Wharf didn't exist for her; only the lapping sounds of the ocean on the pier. She sat there numbly watching the sun set. It was truly a glorious sunset, but Ziven didn't feel a thing.

She didn't see the brilliant orange and yellow turn to deep red and purple, and then fade into various shades of grey. She didn't hear the seagulls calling or even smell the fragrance of sourdough bread and salty ocean in the air.

Suddenly, the fog from the bay had made its way to the pier where Ziven was, and she felt a cold chill shake her entire body. It was dark now, and she needed to get home. It was the Sabbath, and she had not prepared the special meal with Michael... but it was too late now. Nothing could be done.

Perhaps Michael would not be angry with her... perhaps... She carried the tin can with her... not fully realizing that it was still in her hand for it had become as much a part of her as the wooden flute in her other hand had.

Although she tried to remember, she had no recollection of how she actually got home... And when she walked in the door, a relieved Michael took one look at her and invited her into his arms. She buried her face in his embrace and sobbed like a lost child.

<hr>

That night, Ziven didn't sleep at all. She kept tossing and turning and occasionally calling out as a nightmare woke her up. Michael was worried about her. So much so that he could not sleep either. He went into the other room to pray.

Instead of singing his prayer against a wall or facing Jerusalem, he collapsed and fell to his knees to offer a prayer from the depths of his soul. "Most Holy God. God of Abraham, Isaac and Jacob. Creator of all things in the heavens, and all things on earth. Please forgive me, Thy unworthy creation, for coming to Thee for a favor. I am nothing, but Ziven is Thy daughter. She is a golden ray of light among all of Thy creations. She is suffering, and I do not know how to help her. Please guide me and comfort her..."

Michael was not accustomed to praying like that. He had done it once before when he thought Ziven was dead, but he was not used to talking to God as though He were a real person who could hear him and actually answer his prayers.

He had argued doctrine and writings of the Prophets and the Torah... but his prayers were public... so he thought more about what others thought of his prayers, and made sure they were filled with pious words and false humility. Many times he simply recited scriptures from Isaiah or the books of Moses.

He was always so proud that he had memorized such long passages of scripture. Sometimes he just recited something from Psalms and sang it as a prayer. He made sure his melodies were clear and sweet, rather than actually crying unto the LORD.

This time it was different, though. His love for Ziven had grown deeper within him than he thought could ever be possible. It was far more than an aesthetic attraction, though she was beautiful. It was more than chemistry, though there was plenty of that too. It was a oneness between her soul and his that bound them together, much like glue makes two pieces of wood become one solid piece. No longer two... only one.

When she was happy, he was joyful. When she was in pain, he ached desperately. How could he fix this for her? How could he take her pain away? He stayed on his knees for several hours pleading to God for his beloved wife, and actually listening for any answer that might be found.

His silent shouts to the heavens poured out from his soul as it was drawn out of him from someplace within that he had never felt before. He prayed into the wee hours of the morning... until he fell asleep on his knees... not a peaceful sleep, but a very restless sleep.

Chapter XV
Ashes

The next morning was Saturday, so Michael spent the day caring for Ziven. She stayed in bed until almost noon. Her eyes were swollen from crying, but it was truly a cleansing cry. One that cleared out all of the grief from losing her parents and her little girl, and now Atohi – her dear friend. She cried until she had no more tears...

The difference she felt between these tears and any other tears of the past was that she did not feel alone. She did not feel alone in her grief. Somehow, she knew that everything would be alright, and she knew Michael loved her and would be with her always.

She felt nauseous as she tried to get out of bed. *"Must be all of the tears,"* she pondered. She slowly got dressed and made her way to the kitchen where Michael was sketching with pastels. She curiously rounded over to his side of the large canvas to see a beautiful rendering of a Native American woman with bronzed skin, playing a wooden flute on a pier near the ocean at sunset. The fog was beginning to roll in. The sunset was glorious with all of the fiery colors that took your breath away. The Native American woman had an eagle feather with a circle of beadwork tied to a small area of her hair that had been braided, while the rest of her light brown hair was blowing carefree in the breeze behind her. She was wearing a deer-skin dress with long fringe everywhere. Long necklaces of corn beads and other seeds were draped around her neck, hanging to her waist.

The flute in the artwork was a deep brownish-red and had feathers hanging from thin leather straps. It had three stripes near the end, and three stripes near the top. Each was black, white and green.

Ziven had learned that to the Real People, those colors had importance and profound meaning. Black represented strength. Someone who has proven himself in battle with victory could mark himself with black. White represented mourning, but could also represent peace and happiness. Green represented endurance. It is associated with harmony and has great healing power.

The woman was beautiful with a light shining in her features. Her eyes were bright with some gold and a little bit of green in them. Ziven suddenly realized that this was a sketch of her!

She looked at Michael... and he smiled a smile that could only be described as sharing a pure love. Her heart melted as she dissolved into his arms. She felt much better. Michael felt better too, for his smile included a special secret.

Zivan dressed in her Sabbath best, as did Michael. They rode the Trolley Car to Fisherman's Wharf and walked hand in hand to the destined spot with a beautiful ceramic Kiddush cup with a lid Ziven had made that had ribbons of black, red, yellow and white to represent the four directions of the Medicine Wheel.

Michael didn't even count the steps; he was just happy to be with his beloved wife in her time of need. This was a big deal for Michael, and Ziven appreciated this departure from tradition, not only in walking and riding a trolley on the Sabbath, but in participating with her in saying goodbye to her dear friend.

According to Jewish tradition, bodies of the deceased were not to be cremated. That was seen as a desecration. Atohi was not Jewish, but Michael and Ziven had felt that it would show him honor if they held a special ceremony that combined the Jewish and Native American traditions.

This was actually a melding of Ziven's history, and her future, in honor of this man who showed her the way. As the sun began to set and the fog to roll in, Michael offered a beautiful Kaddish prayer, singing the following:

Michael: "May His great Name grow exalted and sanctified..."

Ziven: "Amen."

Michael: "in the world that He created as He willed. May He give reign to His kingship in your lifetimes and in your days, and in the lifetimes of the entire Family of Israel, swiftly and soon."

Ziven: "Amen. May His great Name be blessed forever and ever."

Michael: "May His great Name be blessed forever and ever. Blessed, praised, glorified, exalted, extolled, mighty, upraised, and lauded be the Name of the Holy One, Blessed is He..."

Ziven: "Blessed is He."

Michael: "...beyond any blessing and song, praise and consolation that are uttered in the world."

Ziven: "Amen."

Michael: "May there be abundant peace from Heaven, and life upon us and upon all Israel."

Ziven: "Amen."

Michael: "He Who makes peace in His heights, may He make peace, upon us and upon all Israel."

Ziven: "Amen."

Then, it was Ziven's turn. She opened the lid of the Kiddush cup, and spoke from her heart based upon things she had learned and studied. "Death is a vital tool in the cycle of life. It is like the ocean. It covers Mother Earth and provides new life. It is the place where all knowledge can be drawn to."

"Death is a new beginning and helps us know ourselves through the Four Great Powers of the Medicine Wheel:

The East is the Place of Illumination, where we can see things clearly, far and wide. Its season is spring. Its element is air. Its color is yellow.

The South is the place of Innocence and Trust. Its season is summer. Its element is fire. Its color is red.

The West helps us look within, and speaks to our introspective Nature. Its season is autumn. Its element is water. Its color is black.

To the North is found Wisdom. Its season is winter. Its element is earth. Its color is white.

Oh our Father, the Sky, hear us and make us strong.

Oh our Mother, the Earth, hear us and give us support.

Oh Spirit of the East, purify us with your cleansing winds.

Oh Spirit of the South, may we tread your path.

Oh Spirit of the West, may we always be ready for the long

journey. Even for our own personal Trail of Tears.

Oh Spirit of the North, send us your wisdom.

God, grant us the strength of eagle wings, the faith and courage
to fly to new heights, and the wisdom to rely on His spirit
to carry us there. Amen."

Michael: "Amen."

Then, they joined hands and together slowly poured out the
ashes of Ziven's dear friend into the ocean. "Goodbye my dear friend,"
Ziven cried. "Goodbye."

Then, they held each other for a long time, just listening to the
waves. Their souls seemed to expand beyond themselves and meld into a
oneness that was very healing for both of them. Ziven could see a bright
light envelop them as they held each other. Their auras become one. She
felt complete.

Chapter XVI
Music

Ziven just couldn't get a handle on what was causing her to feel so sick. She was just not herself. She was always tired, but that was probably because she was not sleeping well. She would get up a few times every night to use the bathroom. Certainly, that would explain the fatigue.

That wasn't so bad, it was the nausea that was no fun. It seemed that every smell of food made her head swim and her stomach lurch. Matzah bread wasn't too bad... she could handle that... and it actually seemed to help a little.

Ziven decided that she needed to do something to keep her mind off of her wobbly stomach. So, she pulled out the Bloodwood flute she had made with Atohi.

She stroked the smooth length of the flute, and fingered the hole at its end, checking for any sign of the seam. She had done a good job of sanding. It was very smooth.

She handled the bear-shaped "bird" for the top and used a carving knife to add a little bit of detail. *"There, that should do it."* She threaded the narrow strips of leather through the holes at the base of the "bird" or "fetish."

She had purchased some coconut oil and began to coat the flute to protect it from wear. She rubbed several layers, even being as thorough as to include the finger holes and the end of the flute.

As she rubbed the warm oil on the flute, she began to hum that tune. It was that melody that came from the flute. It was that song that opened the door of communication between Ziven and the Bloodwood flute wide open.

"The woman explained to me that just as I was 'twisted and warped,' she was also 'twisted and warped.' She said that with special care and love she had made me into something beautiful. She explained to me that the Creator, with special care and love, had made her into something beautiful as well. She told me that we were the same! She said that just as she had breathed life into me, and helped me to sing beautiful praises to the Creator... the Creator had breathed life into her and helped her to be able to give back something beautiful... like making a Native American flute. We are the same!"

The flute was complete. Ziven gave thanks to God for the flute and consecrated it to His purposes. She said a silent prayer offering any music it would play to be songs of praise to Him, and of gratitude. She tightened the thin leather straps to press the image of the bear tight to the proper place on the flute. She was about to play it, now that it was finished, but decided to do so at the pier on Fisherman's Wharf where she met Atohi... in his memory.

At the Wharf, Ziven played a melody pure and sweet, yet hauntingly full of emotion. The sound of the notes reverberated off of the water and planks of the pier. The acoustics were surprisingly beautiful.

She had expected the sound to be lost in the menagerie of surrounding noises around her, but it wasn't. She could hear the soul of the flute singing with her.

"She thanked me for allowing her to learn how to do such a beautiful thing and to help me become something I could never have become otherwise. I began to sing... I sang like I had never sung before. I sang a song of praise to the Creator! I sang a song of thanks to be alive!!"

Chapter XVIII
Spring Flowers

Michael could barely hold back his excitement. He had been checking the mail every day for two weeks. He made sure to check it before Ziven had the chance, so she would not find out his secret too early.

He was almost giddy when he saw that a package had arrived. The pink slip from the post office was in the mail, but he quickly slipped it into his pocket before Ziven could see it.

After work, he rode the Trolley to the post office, picked up the package, and excitedly returned home to reveal his surprise. Never before had his commute home seemed so long.

Grinning ear to ear, Michael entered through the front door of their home and called for Ziven. "Darling, are you home? I have a surprise for you!" No answer.

"Ziven... I'm home... are you here?" No answer.

Ziven had not returned from her errands yet. He would have to wait.

He sighed at the prospect and went directly to the kitchen to look for a snack. "Something salty, I think." he said to himself.

He rustled through the pantry looking for some chips or crackers and settled for some microwave popcorn. It seemed a waste and a luxury, but Ziven knew that he liked the kettle corn flavor and would always make sure there was some available for him for moments such as this.

As he poured the newly popped kernels into a bowl, he tried to think of exactly how he would surprise Ziven. He wanted to make it fun. He decided upon a treasure hunt. He decided not to draw a map, but instead to leave a trail of clues making use of some of the American idioms and humor he had been learning.

1. "You are hot stuff" would lead her to the oven.

2. "You clean up nicely" would lead her to the bathroom.

3. "I 'shoes' to be with you forever" would lead her to the shoes in the closet.

4. "Mirror, mirror on the wall, you're the fairest one of all" would lead her to the mirror in the bedroom.

5. "Food is the way to a man's heart" would lead her to the pantry where the package would be hidden.

After hiding all of the notes and the package... he waited for what seemed like an eternity. He felt like a child waiting for his Bar-mitzvah. Eventually, Ziven burst through the front door to find all of the lights off, and Michael sitting on the sofa waiting for her.

"Michael, are you alright?... I'm sorry I'm late." She looked at him quizzically as he motioned for her to join him on the sofa in the darkened room.

Michael just smiled and patted the seat next to him. "What?" Ziven questioned suspiciously as she sat down next to her sweetheart. He was beside himself with excitement as he handed Ziven a little slip of paper with the first clue.

"What is this?" she asked. Raising one eyebrow, he winked and said, "It's the first clue in a treasure hunt for a special surprise."

Ziven jumped up from the sofa and giggling followed the clues until she found the package in the pantry. As she excitedly began ripping away the wrapping paper after opening the shipping box... she suddenly stopped and gasped.

"Oh, Michael! It's beautiful!" she exclaimed. She held up the deerskin dress with long fringe, and ornamental shells, beads and ribbons. The leather was cream colored and extremely pliable and soft to the touch. There were three stripes on each shoulder made from shells, bone fragments, glass beads, and precious stones. The turquoise, tiger eye, and opal caught the dim lights in the house and reflected them magically all around the room as she handled the gift.

There were three colorful stripes at the bottom of the dress made of ribbon, more shells, and bone fragments. The fringe dripping from the arms and collar flowed like a waterfall, dancing around with every movement.

"Put it on," Michael coaxed. "A fashion show?" she teased. "Alright." He didn't have to convince her. The dress was heavy, but not uncomfortable. In fact, it was very comfortable. Ziven could understand why Native American women would wear such a beautiful dress.

She entered the room where Michael was waiting and spun around to watch the fringe flow and the reflections of the gems on the wall and ceiling. "Oh, Michael!" she repeated as she flung herself into his waiting arms and his wide grin.

As she snuggled next to him, fitting comfortably under his arm, she said coyly, "I have a surprise too..."

"What?" his interest peaked.

The only thing Michael liked better than giving surprises, is to receive them. He always worried that this meant he was selfish. Then, he thought about the fun it is to give a surprise, and how he was allowing another person to feel that by receiving the surprise. That quelled his worry and justified his own enjoyment.

"It's a secret," she replied with her head cocked to the side and one eyebrow raised. This was Michael's cue to start a tickling war until Ziven spilled all of the details. Breathless, she conceded, "Okay, okay! I surrender!"

Ziven faced Michael directly, took his face in her hands, and said, "I think you should finish the baby crib. We're going to need it." He had begun to make a baby crib from wood before Batia had passed, but had never finished it.

"What?!" he shouted as he picked Ziven up and spun her around, laughing. The leather fringe of her Native American deerskin dress lifted and flowed freely and gracefully behind them.

"You did it!" he exclaimed. "You did it!"

"God willed it," she said soberly. "Indeed," he replied and kissed her with a long squeeze that told Ziven, Michael was happy. She smiled with a glow and contentment that only comes to a woman with a child who is in love.

"Perhaps I can give him a boy this time," Ziven thought to herself.

Chapter XVIII
Spring Flowers

The winter in San Francisco was rainy and grey. The chill seemed to penetrate to the bone. It was not much colder than winter in Jerusalem, but it was a wet cold. The breeze from the bay seemed to add to the chill, and the evening fog was no help.

Each day, Ziven spent more and more time inside; waiting for spring. It's not that Ziven disliked the winter weather. In fact as the child grew, she was warmed from within. It helped her to look forward to spring. Both because she loved the anticipation of flowers and renewal... and because it meant their daughter would arrive.

She wasn't disappointed that she would be giving Michael a girl. In fact, she thought of the fun she would have dressing her up like a doll. She thought of how she would tell her about the sister she would never meet. She thought of how she would teach her about her Cherokee heritage. She thought of how she would introduce her to the library and instill within her the same love of learning that she, herself, enjoyed.

Spring in San Francisco is much different than spring in Jerusalem. Although the weather is unpredictable, it is a magical time. One should expect any day to include rain and cold wind, then warm sunshine that would draw you to the beach.

In the spring, the entire Bay Area is teaming with spectacular festivals and events that are designed to entice people from all cultures for miles around to endure parking nightmares in order to participate. There is the Japanese Cherry Blossom Festival, San Francisco Bay Carnival, parades, dancers, bands, foot races, and more.

Tourists flood the area and add to the excitement that is already thick in the air. But what Ziven looked forward to most was the flowers. In Jerusalem, it was the blood-red poppies, Bird of Paradise, and delicate white Calla Lillies.

In San Francisco, it is the fragrant Magnolias, the Cherry Blossoms that reminded her of the Almond Tree blossoms in Jerusalem, the delicate Dahlias, and the bright orange California Poppies that spring up everywhere.

San Francisco also seems to make the best use of wild flowers like Purple Chinese Houses that look much like the Wild Iris of Jerusalem only smaller; yellow Violas with their small bright yellow faces; Columbine with its colorful contribution that draw in humming birds; and a myriad of other small flowers of blue, pink, purple, white and yellow. It is truly glorious.

What was surprising to Ziven was the large white flowers of the Yucca plant. It looked like such a sharp-leaved dessert plant, that such a large display of blooms was not expected. Ziven had never seen anything like it.

Another surprise was the "Joshua Tree." Ziven was curious about how such a strange looking cactus got such a biblical name. She did some research and discovered some very interesting information about the "Joshua Tree." It was given that name by a group of "Mormons". Ziven had never heard of "Mormons" before, but put that curiosity to the back burner of her mind for a while.

There was a long list of things that Ziven wanted to research. She didn't exactly know how to research these topics on the Internet, but felt most comfortable using the Encyclopedias at the nearby library.

Michael was better at computers than she was anyway. Ziven looked out the window with her falafel, hummus, Israeli salad (chopped tomato and cucumber), and a pickle. She was sipping on a steaming cup of herb tea (she could never get used to the taste of coffee). She watched the fog literally lift as the sun began to warm up the day.

She looked at the grey clouds and thought to herself, "It will rain again today. How we celebrated the 'rains of blessing' in Jerusalem! Here, rain is common place." She let her mind drift to winter in Jerusalem. When the rains did come, they never dropped vertically with large drenching rain drops like here in San Francisco. The rains were always horizontal with a bitter biting wind. Winter is when the green comes to the hills as the grass gets the long-awaited moisture. Thunderstorms were common in Jerusalem, but were very rare here in San Francisco.

Ziven missed the dramatic clouds and powerful display of God's power through the thunder. Everyone in Jerusalem seemed united when it came to the weather. They were either praying for rain, or giving thanks when it came.

One thing about San Francisco that Ziven did like, though, was the beautiful colors of the changing leaves in the fall. Jerusalem seemed to skip fall altogether. Besides, there were not many trees that changed their color before dropping their leaves.

San Francisco was quite different. The stunning colors of yellow and orange set off the evergreen leaves of the Redwood trees and Cedar trees. It was truly spectacular and never seemed to last long enough.

Ziven didn't miss the dust storms of an Israeli summer, though. And the moisture in the air here made her skin so soft. She never needed lotion to feel like a woman. She was glad they moved here; not just to get away from the bombings... The life she had built here with Michael was good.

She liked the Rabbi at the Mosque near Fisherman's Wharf. He smiled a lot and seemed very knowledgeable. She also liked his voice as he sang the Torah. She wondered if here, in America, it would be permitted for her to read from it herself. That was another question she would add to her list of subjects to find the answers to later.

Some young boys ran past her window. She mused at the difference between their lives, and the reasons they were running, compared to young boys in Jerusalem. Ziven smiled to herself. She had wanted to give Michael a boy – someone to follow in his footsteps.

But they were expecting a girl again. She would, instead, be someone Ziven could give a wonderful opportunity of freedom, education, and meaning to her life. She would teach her the ways of three worlds, Jerusalem, America, and Cherokee. She would teach her to play the Native American flute she had made. She would teach her to keep a proper Sabbath and Passover. And she would teach her how to be an educated contributing member of an American society. This excited Ziven. She couldn't wait for spring to come.

Chapter XIX
The Doctor Visit

"Breast Cancer" was something Ziven had never heard of, so when she heard her doctor say this during one of her routine visits, she didn't know if she should be afraid or not.

Her doctor seemed to be worried since she was six months along in her pregnancy. She asked her to come in again after some test results – and told her to bring Michael with her. Ziven suddenly felt a cold chill run through her body that was not because of the cool temperature in the examining room, nor the lightweight robe with no back she was wearing.

This was very different, and for the first time in her life; Ziven felt truly afraid.

This was saying something, since Ziven had lived through bombings, constant war, and more. This time the fear made her feel like a little child walking in the dark toward the scary unknown, alone.

When Michael got home that evening, Ziven did not know how to tell him. She had been practicing all day, and everything fell flat. She knew he would have a lot of questions that she simply did not know the answers to.

He would want to solve the problem, but this is a problem that cannot be solved... not in one evening anyway. All she needs is a shoulder to cry on, a warm embrace, and the reassurance that everything would be alright and that they would face it together...

Michael had a problem of his own. How was he going to tell Ziven that he got laid off from work that day? How could he possibly look at himself in the mirror and see such a failure? How could he look at his trusting wife who was carrying his unborn child and tell her that he had failed them? How would they pay the bills? What about the cost of medical bills associated with having the baby? Would they have to move? Where could they go? He just shook his head and sighed. Then, he braced himself and entered the doorway of their home.

Ziven wasn't in the kitchen. In fact, she was just sitting in the darkness curled up on the sofa hugging a pillow. She had a blank stare and didn't seem to notice Michael coming in. Something was definitely wrong.

His news would have to wait.

Michael sat next to Ziven and put his arm around her. She didn't move. She just continued to stare straight ahead as though she didn't realize he was even there.

"Maybe something happened with the baby!" he thought to himself. *"What if..."* Then, he stopped himself from spiraling into a panic. His head was pounding, but he knew he couldn't let it show.

"Ziven, Neshama, you know that I love you with all of my soul." He gently touched her cheek and turned her face toward him and looked into her glassy eyes. "You are my Neshama... my soul...What is wrong? How can I help?"

Ziven burst into tears. Not just tears... but sobbing, convulsing cries of sorrow. This brought out a surge of compassion and a desire to protect his beloved. He began to stroke her thick brown hair. This had the effect of calming her and helped her relax. It always did.

Eventually, she stopped crying and looked into his deep brown eyes. They were smooth and black like dark chocolate. They drew her in as though she were hypnotized.

Ziven's breath was still uneven with occasional gasps from crying, but she felt much better. Her head was throbbing, but she felt safe. At least she felt comforted enough to tell Michael about her visit to the doctor earlier that day.

"How much do you know about breast cancer?" she began. Then she drew in another couple of quick breaths and furrowed her brows, looking pleadingly into his face.

Michael could see the fear in her eyes, but he couldn't seem to get rid of the large lump that developed in his throat. "Any kind of cancer is not good," he weakly said.

"I went to the doctor today, and she said to return with you to discuss the possibility that I have..." she could hardly get it out of her mouth... "breast cancer."

Ziven quickly scanned Michael's face to see any trace of what he might be feeling. She knew what she was feeling, but her emotions and thoughts were so loud that she couldn't sense anything else.

"People die from breast cancer. Will I die? I read that chemo-therapy is painful and basically kills as much of your body as possible to try to kill the cancer. People say that is feels like hot lava coursing through the veins and then through the entire body until it is purged out. Then your body has to recover. People get very sick and weak. I wonder if I am going to have to endure that treatment. I'm not looking forward to that! My life has been full of so much pain already...

"I also read that radiation can burn. It basically cauterizes and kills the cancer cells, but it also kills the areas around it just to make sure. Then there are the surgeries. Will I lose my breast? Will I lose both of them? Will I still feel like a woman if that happens? Will Michael's thoughts about me change? Will he still see me as a woman if this does happen?

"What about my unborn child? How will these treatments affect her? What if they choose not to treat me until I give birth? Does that mean that the cancer will continue to grow during that time, and I will have a greater chance of dying? What can be done about this that is safe for my baby? If I die, who will take care of the baby? Who will take care of Michael? I'm so frightened!"

Ziven thought these thoughts all at the same time in one powerful blast of emotion.

Ziven's mind was racing through these thoughts almost simultaneously as she was looking into Michael's eyes, wondering what he was thinking.

Michael was caught off guard. He didn't know what to think. He had never studied cancer, let alone breast cancer. How could he solve this? How could he make things better? He looked into Ziven's eyes, and could see that she was afraid. How could he help her? He said nothing and waited for Ziven to say more when she was ready.

Michael's silence only served to make Ziven's mind go in all sorts of directions and imaginings about what he might be thinking. *"Is he thinking about how I will no longer be a woman? Is he thinking about how difficult it will be for him to feel attracted to me because of this? Is he worried about the baby? Does he even care about what I am facing? Is he going to stop loving me? Will helping me through this be too difficult, and he will leave me? What is he thinking?"*

Finally, Michael asked, "When is your next appointment?" "Wednesday," she answered weakly.

Michael did his best to comfort her. "Everything is going to be alright. You will not have to face this alone. I love you, and nothing will ever change that. You are my soul." Ziven gave a sigh of relief.

He had said just what she needed to hear! They held each other for a long time in the darkness until Ziven finally fell asleep; feeling very safe in Michael's arms. Michael stared ahead into the darkness, not really looking at anything in particular. How could he break it to Ziven about losing his job? How would he be able to pay for medical bills? He could never let her know the stress he was under. She had enough to worry about. He would just have to work it out himself. He needed to be a support for her during this time. JEHOVAH will just have to help him work it out!

He was beginning to feel that JEHOVAH was truly a god of individual caring; that He actually heard and answered prayers; that He was involved in the lives of His children; and that he and Ziven, and their little girl were important to Him.

After a few hours, Michael finally fell into a restless sleep. He dreamed about bill collectors, mounting unpayable bills, Ziven and their new baby girl homeless on the streets...

Certainly, these were nightmares... but Michael's fear was that these things could actually happen if he could not find a new job, and soon.

Chapter XX
Healing on its Wings

One morning, earlier than the light of day had arrived, Ziven was resting in the front room. She looked over at the Bloodwood flute on the mantle of the fireplace. She was thinking about playing it again because she was in a nostalgic mood about Atohi. She wondered what he was doing. Could he still be aware of his existence?

Ziven was not sure exactly what she believed about the afterlife. Orthodox Jewish teachings are not exactly clear on this point. In fact, there are several conflicting philosophies within Jewish Orthodoxy.

Some people taught that the souls of the righteous are reincarnated through many lifetimes. Others taught that the righteous go to a "'heaven" and wait for the Messiah to come; then they will be resurrected. The wicked, however, are supposed to be tormented by creatures of their own creation, or are destroyed upon death and simply cease to exist.

Atohi was certainly a righteous person, so she began to explore her beliefs and thoughts about what his status might be now. *"If there is truly a heaven, surely he would be there,"* she thought to herself. *"If I die, what will happen to me? Will I see my Batia again?"*

In this relaxed state, she felt a presence behind her. It was like warm radiation from an unknown source. She could feel that it was a male. Eventually, she realized that it was Atohi!

She quickly turned around, expecting to see her aged friend, but no one was there. Imprinted on her mind, however, were the following engraved images and conversation instantaneously communicated to her: Atohi was much younger, perhaps in his early 20's. Ziven was surprised that she recognized him because she had never seen him as such a vibrant handsome young man. What helped her recognize him was his soul. She recognized it instantly.

More than that, it was a deeper understanding of who he really was than she had ever experienced with him while he was alive. In this image, Atohi was wearing light-colored ceremonial Native American clothing. His face was glowing, happy and smiling with more than only his mouth... he was smiling with his entire being. Energy seemed to exude from his entire being, from every cell of his body. Energy and light... and love.

He expressed a profoundly deep love for her. He left the impression that he was very happy, but limited in his progression. There was something he needed that he could not do for himself. She wondered what that was, and how she could help. He said not to worry, that she would know when she came across that information.

He told her not to worry, that "everything would be alright." He made it clear that what she was going through would work for her good and be a blessing of healing for her and her family. He also told her to understand that this idea that "everything would be alright" may not be the same result as what she might expect... that it is by the design and timing of the Great Father, and she just needed to trust Him, meaning God.

The next message that Atohi shared with Ziven very clearly, was that she needed to seek for balance in her life, balance with herself, balance with her husband, with nature, and balance with her spiritual connection to the Great Father. Atohi then looked at the Bloodwood flute they had made together and let Ziven know that playing this flute would bring healing to her soul and help her overcome her fears.

Then, there was something about a "Great White Warrior King" that Ziven was supposed to research. This puzzled Ziven. When would she find time to research anything while going through this great trial and emotional upheaval? Atohi was insistent, so she agreed to do this.

That was the end of her experience that lasted a split second. She was left with a warm tingling sensation that seemed to reverberate through every cell of her body. She was even able to sense that the unborn daughter within her was joyful. Ziven smiled in the darkened room.

She got up and reached for the Bloodwood flute. She touched the smooth coolness of the hard wood and tilted it in the darkness. The soft light from the other room seemed to find its way to the flute and illuminate the grain. Ziven put the flute to her lips and began to blow gently. The tone was warm and clear. It was soothing.

She began to play some of the notes she remembered hearing Atohi play. Beautiful peaceful music began to pour out from the flute and into her soul. This peace seemed to flood her heart and mind, then exude around her in a comfortable swirl. She could sense the joy emanating from the flute. Before long, she was feeling very calm and serene. That flute truly was a balm to her troubled soul, and had made her fears vanish... at least for a while.

"I feel joy! I am singing praise to my Creator again! I feel alive! I sing praise! When the woman makes music with me, I feel a connection with her. I can feel her soul. She is afraid. I need to help her somehow. I need to protect her. I can no longer grow or sway with the music of the wind, but I can give her the clearest tones possible. I can help heal her broken heart. I can sing praises to the Creator and perhaps He will help her be happy again."

Ziven took a deep breath. For the first time ever, she paid attention to her lungs taking in the air, and the sensation of her breath hitting her arm. She took another breath. Deeper this time. She paid attention to how it felt for her brain to receive fresh oxygen. Her mind was sharp and clear. Her headache was gone. She absently placed her hands on her swollen stomach, as she often did without realizing it. The girl within her was stretching, her sharp heels threatening to pierce right through the womb.

Ziven didn't mind the pain; it meant her daughter was growing and healthy. *"What will happen to this little one? Will she die too?"* Ziven asked herself. She took another deep breath and silently recited a prayer she had been taught by Atohi:

> *"Oh Great Father who dwells in the sky, lead us to the path of peace and understanding, let all of us live together as brothers and sisters. Our lives are so short here, walking upon Mother Earth's surface, let our eyes be opened to all the blessings You have given us. Please hear our prayers, Oh Great Father."*

She felt at ease. Whatever happens is in the Great Father's hands. She could not change that. She felt a serenity at accepting His will. She knew that everything would be alright as Atohi had promised.

Just then, Michael entered the room. Ziven felt a flood of love for him and rushed into his arms. Surprised at the strength of this emotion from Ziven, he returned the embrace.

After a moment, he braved the question, "Are you ready for today?"

Ziven thought of the pending visit to the doctor to get the results about the suspected breast cancer. She looked into Michael's eyes and forced a smile. "I am ready," she lied.

The truth is, she wanted to be ready, but she was still quite apprehensive. The peace she had experienced gave comfort to her heart, but not to her head. In her head was a battle between trusting in the will of the Great Father, and what the reality of what this illness would mean for her family... and for their daughter.

Chapter XXI
Statistics

Doctor Kikuchi was an Asian woman with a clear complexion, shiny black hair and a petite frame. Her dark slanted eyes twinkled when she spoke. She instantly put Ziven and Michael at ease with a gentle smile.

The first thing Dr. Kikuchi said was, "Have you researched breast cancer on the Internet?" Michael and Ziven answered together, "Yes. Of course." Dr. Kikuchi continued, "I'm not going to sugar-coat it." Michael and Ziven looked at each other with a puzzled look. "That means, that I am not going to lie to you to make it easier to accept," Dr. Kikuchi clarified for them.

"We need to discuss the treatment options first, then the consequences, and finally make a decision as to which course to take. This could take some time, so let's begin by talking about the tests."

Michael and Ziven nodded in understanding. "After a physical examination, it is clear that you have a lump in your left breast. It is about the size of a grape. It is thick but it is not consistent in shape. This concerns me because, if it is cancer, the chances are that it has metastasized or spread to other parts of the body. There are treatments to account for this, which we will discuss."

"Does this make sense so far?" Ziven and Michael nodded. "Okay, so the first thing I'd like to do is to order a diagnostic mammogram. This will give us a clear picture of the size, shape, and density of the mass. We should also be able to see if it is just a cyst or something more serious."

They didn't know what a "mammogram" was, but submitted like little children anyway. After the test, they waited for the doctor to review the results. It seemed like ages, but it was only about 30 minutes.

Michael asked, "Did it hurt?"

"No," Ziven replied. She had never had a mammogram before and was surprised at how thin the panels of the machine could squeeze and spread her breasts. It was extremely uncomfortable, but not exactly painful. The female technician was very sensitive to Ziven's discomfort in having a woman, and stranger, handling her breasts. She looked away as often as possible and provided Ziven with as much modesty as she could.

Dr. Kikuchi returned, but did not have a smile on her face. She hesitated. Ziven could sense that it was difficult for her to continue. "It doesn't look good," she began. "I recommend a test to see if you have the gene for breast cancer. If you do, we will most likely need to do a double mastectomy. If you do not, we will only need to worry about the left side. Do you have any questions at this point?"

"What is a 'mast-ect-omy'," Ziven asked hesitantly.

"That is when we surgically remove the entire breast."

Michael said, "Let's wait until we get the results from this next test before we make any other decisions." Ziven wondered at Michael's quick response and had to push away thoughts about what he might be feeling about her as a woman if her breasts were removed.

"Agreed," Dr. Kikuchi continued. "Once the results are in, come see me again and we'll go from there. But I must tell you that I suspect that we should move quickly on this one. There is a certain sense of urgency. Are you alright?"

"I don't know how to answer that," Ziven answered. "I feel sort of numb."

"That's normal. There is a lot to take in at once. We'll do all we can and will try to answer all of your questions as they arise."

Ziven nodded and weakly smiled.

"Now, after the blood test... try to get some rest. You're going to need it," the Asian doctor concluded and left the room.

The blood test was uneventful, and Michael and Ziven would have to wait for results again. This time they would have to wait four weeks before the results returned from a lab somewhere. They made another appointment to meet with Dr. Kikuchi at that point.

Ziven appeared to be calm on the outside, and Michael was surprised. His mind was racing, the stress building. He had not told her that he lost his job yet. That was one stress. How bad is this cancer and what will it take to save Ziven's life? The treatments all sound horrible. They basically take her as close to death as possible hoping to kill the cancer, then try to revive her health slowly afterward.

Michael had picked up a brochure about breast cancer during their last visit to the doctor's office. He learned that the death rate is one in every thirty-six. Over 12% of women in the United States contract breast cancer annually. That means over 40,000 women in the United States die of breast cancer every year. These were terrible statistics, and he didn't want Ziven to be one of them!

He looked over at his wife as they rode the BART home. How calm she seemed, he thought to himself. *"She must be terribly upset, but she won't share that with me. She doesn't share anything with me anymore. She keeps her feelings close to me. I'm not sure she loves me anymore.*

"What about the baby? How will the treatments affect her? I don't know if we can endure the loss of another child! It almost broke Ziven last time, and our marriage suffered as well. I don't think we could recover from it.

"How will I ever pay for the medical bills without a job? I am such a failure as a provider! I have failed my family! I have failed JEHOVAH! I don't see any solution. I will just need to work even harder to find a job, but who will hire a failure? I have failed everyone!"

Ziven sensed the tenseness in Michael. Didn't he know that everything would be alright? *"I guess I never shared with him the peace I found,"* she considered.

"Atohi came to me and said everything would be alright." Ziven spun her head around to look at Michael. Had she actually said that out loud? Michael was looking at Ziven in surprise. She HAD said it out loud. She scanned her feelings to try to sense what he felt about that, so she could decide whether to tell him more or not.

Michael closed his eyes and shook his head. He had no idea what Ziven was talking about, but he had too much on his mind to spend time trying to figure it out. How was he going to solve his problems? He felt so helpless to resolve Ziven's situation. The only thing he could do was find another job, and soon. Even that was something he had little control over. Everything seemed to be out of his control. He felt entirely helpless.

Ziven saw his response as a direct reaction to her comment about Atohi. This made her feel sad and alone. She concluded that she could not trust him to be her supportive friend throughout this ordeal. She would have to rely on the Great Father. She would have to find peace playing her flute and remembering the few good moments of her life.

Atohi had told her to find balance with all things. She didn't know how she was going to find balance with Michael. *"I'll do my best to be balanced in all other things, and worry about peace with Michael later,"* she thought. She made sure this time that she did not verbalize her thoughts. Not yet anyway.

Chapter XXII
Drinking from the Firehose

The four weeks seemed to inch forward slowly, but eventually the time did come. Michael and Ziven found themselves in Dr. Kikuchi's office again.

"The test results were negative."

Ziven gasped.

Doctor Kikuchi quickly said, "No, negative in this case is good! It means that you do not have the cancer gene that would require a double mastectomy." There was no response.

Michael and Ziven looked at each other and then back at the doctor.

"This is good news," the doctor continued. Then she pulled out a book with graphic pictures of surgeries, reconstruction surgeries, and worse-case scenarios. Ziven could hardly look at the gore, but Michael had seen worse in war zones and during bombings, so it didn't seem to bother him at all. "I just want to give you all of the facts so you can make an educated decision," Dr. Kikuchi explained.

"During the surgery, we will remove the affected area as well as some of the tissue surrounding it. We will then take a biopsy of one of your lymph nodes and test it for cancer. If it is free of cancer cells that will make things much easier. If it is not, we will discuss the next steps from there. Do you have any questions about this part?"

Ziven finally spoke up and asked, "Is there any danger to my baby?"

"There is always some risk with anesthesia, but you are in good hands, and we will take every precaution to safe-guard your child as well as you." Then she smiled. Ziven trusted her.

This put her at ease, but Michael seemed to be a million miles away. He didn't seem to be paying attention. Ziven wasn't sure he cared about what was happening to her. She couldn't read him at all.

Dr. Kikuchi continued, "As for the Chemotherapy, well, we will cross that bridge when we come to it. And the radiation... we will take the proper precautions. I really feel that we should act quickly. I'd like to admit you immediately and schedule surgery for the first thing tomorrow morning.

"We will not know exactly how much of the tissue will have to be removed until we get in there. You need to prepare for the worst and hope for the best."

Michael didn't stay the night at the hospital. He made some excuse and left as quickly as he could, saying that he would be back in the morning. Ziven was left alone to deal with the cold tile floor, the tall bed, the lightweight "robe" with funny ties and an opening in the back. The temperature in the room was far too cool for her comfort, and the blankets were thin.

Occasionally, a nurse would bring her a thin blanket that had been heated. That was nice, but the comfort wore off quickly, and she was shivering again. She summoned all of her courage to remain calm and to maintain a positive attitude. That night, the little sleep she was able to get was restless and filled with nightmares. The images of reconstruction surgery that removes muscle, skin and tissue from the back or thigh kept replaying in her mind. The procedure that stretches the pectoral muscle to lift it in preparation for the additional muscle sounded painful.

Then, there was Michael... he was not supportive. She had to face this alone. That seemed to be the most frightening part of her nightmares.

Ziven sat up in bed and woke with a start, breathing heavily, sweating, frightened. In her nightmare, she and Michael were standing on a cliff overlooking the crashing waves of the ocean below. Ziven was thinking about how romantic it was and leaned in to kiss him, when he pushed her off the cliff. As she was falling, she could hear him laughing!

"What a horrible nightmare!!" Then, as her breathing returned to normal, she pondered this question, *"Why isn't Michael here to be with me, especially now? Has he stopped loving me?"*

As Michael waited for Ziven to return from the surgery, he decided he should tell her about losing his job. He didn't know how she would react, and certainly this was not a good time to add anything to her worries, but he knew she would be upset if he didn't tell her soon. He just couldn't keep that big a secret from her any longer. It was killing him inside.

When they wheeled Ziven's bed back into the room where Michael was waiting... she was just coming out of the effects of the anesthesia. She was groggy and slightly silly, as if she were inebriated. Michael smiled as he decided not to tell her yet since she would never remember anything he said until she was entirely awake anyway.

"I'm so glad you're here," Ziven slurred. Her mouth was dry, and she felt a little nauseous. "You are my favorite one of all," she said. Michael laughed.

"Did you bring my Bloodwood flute? I so wanted to hear you play it for me... It would make all of the little children follow you," she slurred.

"Where did those animals on the ceiling come from?" She giggled.

Then she began singing a song with words that were not really words... only slurry sounds. "Oh! There is a seagull!" she said just before slowly closing her eyes and letting her head drop to the pillow.

Then, she raised both eyebrows high as she struggled to open her eyes. "I'm so thirsty!" she mumbled, licking her lips. Michael shook his head and smiled as he reached for some ice chips for his bride. But before he could give them to her, she had slipped into a groggy sleep.

A little while later, she slowly woke up. Ziven began speaking with someone that Michael could not see. She wasn't making any sense to him, but she seemed alert and animated as she was speaking gibberish. "Did you see Atohi?" she asked Michael, her eyes bright and clear. He shook his head, and her countenance fell. "Well, he was here, and he told me that I was not to worry... everything will be alright," she smiled broadly.

Michael sat on the bed near her feet, took her hand, and asked... "Are you alright?"

"I'm fine!" she beamed. She seemed to be alert and fully aware.

Michael assessed her condition and determined that she was fully cognizant and awake. It was time to tell her. He drew in a deep breath and gathered the courage to begin. "I have some bad news," he muttered with his head down. He couldn't meet her now penetrating gaze. He decided to just come out with it at once, and receive her rebuke afterward, rather than trying to explain and lead up to the dreadful news.

"I lost my job. I have failed you; I know..." Ziven interrupted him.

"You have never failed me. Look at me..." She took his face in her hands and waited for him to look into her eyes. "Listen to me... You could never disappoint me. You are not a failure!"

Michael broke away and stood up. "You don't understand!" He began pacing. "I...I can't pay the hospital bills. I did nothing wrong, but I was released without any notice or reason. I have been looking for a new job every day since then. I have been deceiving you! You thought I was going to work, but I was looking for a new job. It's been over a month now."

Breathing a sigh of relief after having spilled out all of his burden as fast as he could, he looked at Ziven – much like a lost puppy.

"Oh, Michael! Everything will be alright! I've been promised this!" Michael wasn't so sure. "I've got to go. I'll pick you up tomorrow." He left without saying another word.

Chapter XXIII
The Great White Warrior King

Ziven was at home now, but unable to get out of bed much. The doctors had told her to remain in bed for 3 weeks. She felt guilty that she couldn't prepare meals for Michael, but he didn't seem to mind much. He would bring her soup from a can, and bread from a store.

Even though the very thought of eating was a burden to her, she would dutifully eat the food he would bring each day. He was still distant, but would bring her books from the library on topics she requested. Usually, they were about Native Americans.

As Ziven read about more about the Trail of Tears, she began to equate her life to a personal Trail of Tears:

* Growing up in an orphanage that stank in the summer and froze in the winter.

* Being teased by children who didn't understand her.

* The women who made fun of her when they didn't know she was there.

* Being invisible to her family.

* Being caught between two worlds.

* The bombing and unrest of Israel.

* The bomb that killed her parents and left her trapped under rubble.

* Troubles with Michael and his indifference to her.

* Fear of flying since the incident while coming to America.

* Leaving her home and starting all over again without any friends.

* Losing her firstborn daughter; sweet Batia.

* The Diabetic Coma.

* The death of Atohi.

* And now, breast cancer, its treatments and risks, the danger to her baby and her own life.

* And, on top of it all.... Michael's continued indifference to her... She had to face everything alone.

Ziven, in contemplating her own "Trail of Tears" began to feel deeply depressed. Her breathing began to be irregular, her eyebrows to furrow, and tears began to burn her eyes. Then, she remembered the visit by Atohi. She began to think of the good things that have happened in her life, i.e. the love of Ima and Abah, the day she found out she was Cherokee, finding comfort in the arms of a Carob tree, meeting Michael, hearing the songs of all living things, safely making it to America, talking to the Redwood trees, stepping into the ocean and feeling the sand escape from beneath her feet, feeling the life within the vastness of that ocean, being able to see glorious sunsets and feel the energy of a thunderstorm, her near-death experience, the feeling of a new life growing within her, walking along Fisherman's Wharf, meeting Atohi, communicating with and making the Bloodwood flute, playing its soothing music... There were more good memories than she thought.

She remembered the good times she had with Michael and tried to make them overshadow the distance they now felt. She tried to remember the things she was told to research, but her mind was numb. *"I'll think about that later,"* she reassured herself.

Among the books Michael brought her was a book about the ancient Americas. It spoke of bloodthirsty people who delighted in bloodshed and war amongst each other. This reminded her of her Arab brothers and their centuries of warring with each other and Israel. She felt she understood what it must have been to grow up during that time period.

The Aztec people were very artistic. They loved poetry, sculpting, drawing, and covered their bodies with tattoos to honor their warriors for their accomplishments. They enjoyed team sports. Their favorite game was Ullamaliztli. The team hit a rubber ball with their heads, elbows, knees and hips without letting it touch the ground. The object was to get the rubber ball through a small stone ring. "Interesting," she thought.

The Aztec children were educated in schools. There were different schools for girls and for boys. Even among the boys, there was a different education for boys of nobility. The common boys were trained for war, while the noble boys were trained in history, astronomy, art, and how to govern or lead. Girls were taught how to make a pleasant home.

Ziven thought about her own childhood and how she longed for a proper education. The boys were taught from the books of Moses and from the Torah. They were encouraged to argue points of doctrine.

They were taught about politics, science, and math. They were free to learn anything they chose to.

The girls were not. They were expected to learn about how to be good homemakers, how to make lace, how to cook, and how to prepare for the holidays. There were so many similarities between the Jewish history of her past, and these Native Americans of ancient times, it was stunning.

The Aztecs were thought to have been killed off mostly by disease, not by war. She had read that the Cherokee and other Native American tribes were also affected by disease. Interesting similarity.

The Aztecs were named so by the Westerners who took it from one of the original places the Aztecs lived around the 12th century. They actually referred to themselves as Mexica. This is where the name for the country of Mexico originally came from.

Ziven pondered upon that concept for a moment. It must be difficult for a people to not be able to keep their own name for themselves... their identity is essentially wiped clean by another group of people. The meaning of who they are and where they come from, erased by those who do not appreciate the history and culture of the other group of people. Sad.

The Aztec/Mexica people had their own language. It was an advanced system for keeping records and was a form of picture writing. Records were kept on deerskin or paper made from bark. They would write with charcoal and then color the writing with vegetables and other substances. Their writings were very specialized and only performed by the learned.

They kept tax records, historical records, information about religious sacrifices and other ceremonies. They wrote poetry and put their writings together in books. Sometimes, they even wrote their most precious records on sheets of metal they had pressed or hammered into thin flat plates.

Ziven thought of her own Cherokee people and the language they developed that had interested her. The similarities between her people and this ancient civilization were amazing. There were other practices by the Aztec/Mexica people that were bloodthirsty and horrific, i.e. human sacrifice and selling their children into slavery. These were difficult for Ziven to imagine.

Atohi said that the Native American people were bloodthirsty anciently. This is not something to be proud of. Then, there was the story of the Great White God, Quetzalcoatl, who visited the Aztec/Mexican people as well as Mayan people sometime near the center of time. This man was of "comely appearance and serious disposition. His countenance was white, and he wore a beard. His manner of dress consisted of a long, flowing robe." Interesting. Is this "Great White God" the "Great White Warrior King" Atohi had told her to investigate?

Quetzalcoatl was recognized as the creator of all things, born of a virgin, and performed miracles among the people. He taught the ordinance of baptism, prophesied of future events and taught the people to stop worshipping many gods. There was a new star associated with Him and His coming. There was recorded a great destruction just before His coming, and His symbol was a cross. Quetzalcoatl sent out disciples to preach His message and He promised that he would return a second time.

He was associated with the bread of life, assisted the dead, died on a tree while shedding his blood to save the fate of mankind. He was associated with light and the sun, and was resurrected and played a role in the rebirth of the deceased. He taught that His children will become lords and heirs of the earth.

Interesting... this sounded a lot like the stories she had heard about the great prophet Jesus of Nazareth that Christians believe was the Messiah. Of course, the Jews believe that he was not. They still wait for the Messiah to come and bring the world political peace.

Ziven thought about this for a moment. She wondered, *"Did a Great White God really appear to the people of the ancient Americas... and if so, who was He? If the Quetzalcoatl was resurrected, could He not have visited the ancient civilization of the Aztec/Mexica and Mayan people? He could do anything... right?*

"And what of this Jesus? The Christians say He was resurrected too. If He was... could the Quetzalcoatl actually be Him? I don't know," thought Ziven to herself.

"This is a lot to assimilate. I'm not sure I want to abandon my Jewish customs completely, whether for my Native American heritage, or for the Christian traditions."

Ziven decided to try to find the information on the Internet. She searched for "similarities between Quetzalcoatl and Jesus"... and found many interesting articles that seemed to tie the two together.

There was even an article that said an ancient record of that event had been preserved on metal pages. It was translated and used as scripture for that religion she had heard of before, the "Mormons." She had too much on her mind to spend any more time trying to figure this out. Far too much on her mind. Besides, Michael would be home from his job search soon, and she needed to gather her strength to prepare the evening meal for him.

Chapter XXIV
Decisions

Ziven and Michael found themselves at the doctor's office again to discuss the options and next steps. Although the surgery was a success, and only a single mastectomy was necessary, it was nonetheless a complete removal of her left breast.

Ziven's wound was still seeping and painful. Although she didn't want to take any pain medications, she hated to admit that they did help a little. She hurt each time she moved. She was surprised at how often that was... It wasn't easy to explain, so she didn't try. Besides, she and Michael had barely said two words to each other since she got out of the hospital three weeks ago. This saddened her deeply, but there was nothing she could do about it.

"I can't think about that now. I need to focus on what the Dr. Kikuchi is saying."

"...Chemotherapy would be dangerous for the baby, so you'll have to make a decision about that."

"What? What decision?!" Ziven countered vehemently.

"If you choose to undergo the Chemotherapy, it will most likely kill your unborn child, or she will be born with terrible handicaps i.e. blindness, mental retardation, and deformed limbs and probably never walk or have children. On the other hand, if you choose to end this pregnancy, you can avoid all of this."

Ziven couldn't believe what she was hearing! That wasn't even a choice!

Dr. Kikuchi continued, "If you do not choose to go through the chemotherapy treatments, the cancer could very likely return, and we won't know where it will land in your body. The chances of your survival in that case are very slim."

Ziven looked at Michael. He was looking down at his hands, cleaning his fingernails. "Was he even listening?!!"

Dr. Kikuchi persisted, "Because of the fast-moving cancer you had, we need to start right away with the radiation we talked about." Ziven looked up, startled.

"Don't worry. We'll take all of the precautions we can to protect your baby. We have a lead apron to cover and protect your abdomen," the doctor explained. "You will be required to undergo a series of treatments, with time in between for you to recover and regain your strength. Does that make sense?"

Ziven nodded, then looked over at Michael... He was still looking down. "You should also know that your hair will fall out, and you will feel very tired for a few days after each treatment. Your sense of taste will change. You will taste a metal flavor in your mouth and that will affect your pallet. You will not feel like eating, but you will need to eat anyway to keep up your strength... Here is a booklet with all of the information you will need. Do you have any questions?"

Ziven answered, "Michael and I need a moment to discuss this decision."

"Of course," Dr. Kikuchi said. "I'll be back in a moment." She left and closed the door quietly behind her.

Ziven turned to Michael, "I don't know what's going on with you, but this is important! We need to make a decision about this." Michael looked at Ziven weakly as though he hadn't heard anything she was saying.

Ziven repeated, "Dr. Kikuchi says I need to undergo radiation. She also said that we need to decide if I should have chemotherapy. If I don't, that means I could die... or she thinks we should have an abortion... If I have the Chemotherapy, it could hurt our daughter and cause her to be either killed, or terribly deformed!"

Michael answered, "I can't make a decision like that! When we lived in Jerusalem, maybe, but things have changed... And I am such a failure, I can't trust any decision I would make anyway." Then he stood up and said, "You do what you want," and walked out.

Ziven was dumbfounded. She couldn't believe what had just happened! Dr. Kikuchi returned to find Ziven crying. "I know this is difficult. What did you decide to do?" she asked. Ziven summoned all her courage to say, "I will undergo the radiation, but not the Chemotherapy... at least, not until after the baby is born."

"Are you sure? You understand the risk to yourself?"

Yes. I understand. My mind is made up."

Chapter XXV
The Healing Flute

The long days progressed with the patterns of a few days of relative strength, and then several days of extreme exhaustion and miserable pain. Ziven's hair fell out by the handful. She became very depressed. Not only that, but Michael's indifference felt like rejection.

Sometimes it was more than she could bear. The only comfort Ziven felt was when she played the Bloodwood flute. The warm resonating melodies that flowed from it were certainly soul soothing. Regardless of the agony her body was going through, the emotional torture of living in the same house with someone who seemed to despise her, and the worry about her unborn child, she found peace in the connection with this flute; her only friend.

As she played sweet melodies, she could feel it communicating with her a joyful praise to the Creator/Great Father. She sensed that it wanted to help heal her troubled soul. She began to join in with singing praise. She found herself playing it every morning with the sunrise and every night with the setting sun.

Ziven decided to try to teach Michael to play the Bloodwood flute. Perhaps it would ease his mind about things. Perhaps it could bring them closer together. Perhaps it could heal his soul as it had healed hers.

She explained it to him this way: "I'd really like to share something with you. It would mean so much to me if you would try to play this Bloodwood flute. I really feel it will help you and bring peace to your soul, as it does mine. But first, there is a story I'd like to share with you.

"My people, the ancient Native Americans, were a bloodthirsty people. They were wicked and loved war and bloodshed. Then, one day a leader arose from among my people who could speak with The Great Father. The Great Father told these leaders to write down the record of my people. The Great Father promised that He would send His Son to my people. He promised that His Son was the light, and that He would come to save the world from the darkness.

"The Great White Warrior King DID come to my people in the ancient Americas. They heard His voice. They saw His face. They felt the prints in His hands and His side, and in His feet." Michael jerked his head up and looked at her.

Ziven continued, "He taught them how to love. The Great White Warrior King brought peace to my people and healed them from their bloodlust. There was peace among my people for a very long time afterwards. He promised that He would return, so my people wait. Just like the Jews, we wait for a Prince of Peace. We both wait. We are the same.

"The Jews praise God with music. The Native American people also praise God with music. We are the same.

"When I made this Native American flute from the wood of a Bloodwood tree, I felt it teach me a lesson. It was once part of a living thing, but was cut off; just like we were with the God of heaven, but were cut off as we came to earth and sin. The flute taught me that with great and tender care, we can be made into something beautiful in His hands, just as the flute was crafted into something beautiful. And, finally, as I breathe into this flute, it gives back a beautiful song of praise to the Creator. This is the same as how the breath of life helps us become something more, that can give back beauty to all those around us."

Ziven studied Michael's face to see if she could detect how he felt about everything she had just shared with him. She expected him to raise his voice and demand that she sticks to being a Jew and forget all of the silly Native American traditions. She avoided the urge to prod him and simply waited patiently.

Finally, Michael simply said, "You believe what you want." He grabbed his jacket and briefcase, and left without saying another word. Ziven bowed her head and began to pray as she had never prayed before.

Chapter XXVI
Esther

Michael sat alone in the darkened room staring blankly out the window. He hadn't moved for seven hours. The news about Ziven was such a surprise that he was certainly in shock. He was replaying the last 24 hours in his mind. Ziven had collapsed. Michael called 911 and rode in the ambulance with her, holding her hand and regretting the last words he had said to her. He also felt guilty about not keeping his promises to be a loving support for her. *"This can't be the end!"* he lamented. *"I need the chance to make it up to her!"*

He kept checking the large clock on the wall over and over again; agonizing over every minute that passed. *"Two minutes?! It's only been two minutes?"* Then his mind, dulled with the overload of emotion, turned off. He just sat there, hunched over with his eyes half open, glassy, and staring blankly at his knee.

Waiting in the reception area seemed interminable. Finally, the doctor came out with a long face and sat down next to him. She gently touched his arm until he realized she was there and looked up into her sad eyes.

Dr. Kikuchi looked down briefly, drew in a long breath and began. "I am so sorry to tell you this. We did everything we could for her."

"What!!! What has happened?" He managed to get out.

"I am so sorry, but Ziven is gone. We were able to save the baby, but your wife has passed away."

Michael was obviously in shock, so the doctor directed him to the local chapel so he could be alone in his grief. Finally, after several hours, Michael emerged from the chapel with red puffy eyes and a dejected posture. He found a nurse and asked about where his child might be. He was directed to an area of the Neonatal Intensive Care Unit where his daughter was in a small bed with a plastic lid covering her.

There was a bright bluish-white light shining on her little body when he came to the window. A nurse motioned for him to come in. He scrubbed his hands with foaming soap and a little sponge that had little bristles on the other side. He wore paper coverings over his shoes, on his hair, over his beard, and a jumpsuit over his clothes.

They put special gloves on his hands and told him he could finally enter the room where his daughter lay fighting for her life. He was amazed that her little veins would be large enough for such huge needles and tubes. Her skin was almost transparent and he could see the pattern of blue and red lines crisscrossing underneath.

Michael watched as his little daughter's small chest would rise and fall with quick little breaths. She was sleeping with her hands above her head and her legs bent and lying with her knees flat against the bed. She weighed only 5 pounds 6 ounces and wore only a little diaper that was pinned loosely around her waist.

Electronic probes were stuck to her abdomen and chest, no doubt the cause for all of the beeping machines surrounding her tiny body. She looked like a little doll in size. He loved her immediately.

Emotion swelled up inside him and he quickly wiped away a flood of tears. He thought he had cried all of the tears his eyes would ever have... but here they were again. *What if she dies too?!!*" he shouted within himself.

If she did survive, it would be at least 2 weeks before he could bring her home. Even then, it would be a risky situation. She would have to return to the hospital often so she could be put in a bed with the same bright blue lights he had seen to counteract the bilirubin of her yellow skin until her kidneys began to work properly.

"How can I survive without Ziven!" Michael said out loud as he put his face in his hands and began to sob. A compassionate nurse put her hand on his shoulder, and motioning to the other infants in the room said, "All of these little ones are surrounded by angels. Can you feel it?"

Michael gained his composure and looked around. The room was filled with beds with plastic covers like the one his precious daughter was in. They each had two large holes on each side to allow adult hands to enter to take care of the needs of the little ones.

Many of the babies were much smaller than his daughter. Some were even the size of a chipmunk... barely large enough to fit in one's hand. There were some parents near some of the children... some reaching in and cooing to their infants, and others actually holding and rocking their babies.

Michael felt a strange peacefulness in the room. The beeping machines seemed to be drowned out by the overwhelming and thick, warm, calm that permeated the room and soaked into his very bones.

Although the lights in the room were dim, it was as though the areas around each child was surrounded by an intense and peaceful light.

Michael had never felt, nor sensed anything like that before. Perhaps there really were angels around these little ones. Perhaps angels were surrounding his own precious daughter. Perhaps his beloved Ziven was there... Perhaps.

Michael turned slowly to the nurse and asked if he could reach in and touch his daughter. The nurse smiled and nodded "Of course." His hand reached in slowly through the hole in the side of the plastic lid of the incubator.

As his finger stroked her little arm and made its way to her little hand, she clasped it in a reflex. Michael felt a warm chill race throughout his body that left him feeling such awe at the wonder of it all. He felt the terrible emptiness within him begin to heal as he communed with the soul of this little one.

He thought he heard within his head (or was it his heart), a whisper from Ziven saying, "Everything will be alright. I will watch over you both. Teach her about me. Teach her about being Jewish and Cherokee."

<hr>

The day finally came when Michael could bring his daughter home. He had to choose a name for the birth certificate before she could be released. He remembered Ziven telling him about how she wished she were like Queen Esther. He decided to name her Esther Ziven in honor of her mother.

He knew he would have a heavy task in front of him, carrying for a newborn baby by himself, especially with her health problems. "What do I know about raising a baby?" he exclaimed. That first night was so difficult. Esther cried for several hours. Michael tried to feed her warm infant formula every 2 hours as he had been instructed, but nothing seemed to work. He rocked her. He sang to her. He walked with her. He swayed and bumped her up and down. He tried swinging her back and forth. He was exhausted.

It's a good thing he didn't have a job, so he could care for her... but then, not having a job meant he couldn't pay the medical bills, nor purchase all of the things a new baby needs, like diapers, formula, blankets, warm clothing, etc.

He discovered a parent services program nearby that helped with the cost of food, and a discount store that offered parenting classes and gave credits towards all of the other things he would need. *"What a blessing from The Great Father!"* he thought to himself.

He mused that he now called the God of Abraham, Isaac, and Jacob "The Great Father." Perhaps some of what Ziven had told him had become part of him after all. Perhaps that was one way he could keep her memory alive. He wondered if there really was a heaven, and thought, *"Surely, if there is a heaven, my Ziven would be there... I wonder what she is doing right now, and if she is aware of us."*

One day, he noticed the Bloodwood flute on the mantle and remembered that last day, when Ziven had tried to teach him to play it. He carefully took the flute in his hands and tilted it back and forth in the sunlight that was streaming through the window. The shimmering golden grain was beautiful.

Michael put the flute to his mouth and blew a soft steady stream of air. The sound emanating from the Native American flute was warm and mellow. He moved his fingers up and down the flute and was surprised at how easy it was to play.

Suddenly, Esther was cooing. She was soothed by the sound. Michael had found the magic cure. He began playing the flute every morning and evening. Not just because it soothed Esther, but because it was also beginning to heal his own soul.

As Esther grew, she loved to hear Michael play the Bloodwood flute. One day, she asked about it. Michael knew this day would come. That didn't make it any easier, but he was determined to try.

Michael became the storyteller... he told Esther of her mother's trail of tears... and courage... and faith. He pondered about how different their life would have been if they had stayed in Jerusalem... a very different life indeed.

He had read Ziven's journals and felt as though he could explain how she felt about her Cherokee heritage, and all of the things she had learned about that part of her culture. Michael also felt it important to teach Esther about Jewish traditions and culture. He also decided to teach her how to be a good American. "Interesting," he thought to himself, "how Ziven seems to have gotten the last word after all." He smiled to himself as he imagined Ziven in heaven laughing.

As he looked at his daughter, he could see Ziven's eyes... those beautiful hazel eyes that were sometimes green and sometimes golden in the sun. She had her mother's hair and spirited nature. He loved her more than he ever thought it possible to love again.

It wasn't because she reminded him of Ziven... but that was certainly part of it. It was because she was part of him, and part of Ziven. Something they created together that would help keep his bride alive even though she was no longer with them... not physically anyway.

Then one day, years later, Michael would teach Esther how to play the Bloodwood flute. The circle would complete and the thought of that made him feel balanced. Everything would be right after all... just as Ziven had said.